THE
MILITIA
HOUSE

THE
MILITIA
HOUSE

A Novel

JOHN MILAS

Henry Holt and Company
New York

Henry Holt and Company
Publishers since 1866
120 Broadway
New York, New York 10271
www.henryholt.com

Library of Congress Cataloging-in-Publication Data

Names: Milas, John, author.
Title: The militia house : a novel / John Milas.
Description: First edition. | New York : Henry Holt and
    Company, 2023.
Identifiers: LCCN 2022052764 (print) | LCCN 2022052765
    (ebook) | ISBN 9781250857064 (hardcover) |
    ISBN 9781250857071 (ebook)
Subjects: LCGFT: Horror fiction. | War fiction. | Novels.
Classification: LCC PS3613.I4754 M55 2023 (print) |
    LCC PS3613.I4754 (ebook) | DDC 813/.6—
    dc23/eng/20221221
LC record available at https://lccn.loc.gov/2022052764
LC ebook record available at https://lccn.loc.gov/2022052765

Our books may be purchased in bulk for promotional,
educational, or business use. Please contact your local
bookseller or the Macmillan Corporate and Premium Sales
Department at (800) 221–7945, extension 5442, or by e-mail at
MacmillanSpecialMarkets@macmillan.com.

First Edition 2023

Designed by Devan Norman

Printed in the United States of America

10 9 8 7 6 5 4 3 2 1

FOR JAMES BODDY

There were no roads in the Helmand Province in 2010,
except for the Ring Road, which didn't go to any
of the places we needed to get to.
—JEFF CLEMENT

Let us begin with the bad little specimen.
—NICKI MINAJ

THE
MILITIA
HOUSE

I

I

A dog walks up to the guard post with half its face stuck full of porcupine quills. We hear it stumbling in the gravel behind us. Blount gasps when the red light of his moonbeam finds the black-and-white quills in the side of the dog's face. All I can think in the moment is this: I am not a compassionate person. I didn't come here to help, not people and not dogs. The needles are twice the length of a pencil, clustered hideously across the side of a furry white face. Some of the quills have barely missed an eye. Then a cloud of flies swarms into the guard post. They buzz and whine in our ears. We're used to the flies here, but this is more than usual. Blount raises a gloved hand and swats them out of his face. I hold my M16 steady with one hand and use the other to swat flies away. This is our first night on duty in Kajaki.

The dog looks from me to Blount and then back to me as if there's still something we could do to help. But if we weren't getting attacked by bugs right now, it's not like we have a vet hospital here. FOB Z, where we live, doesn't have a clinic for hurt dogs. Most FOBs don't, probably not even Camp Leatherneck or Delaram II. And you don't get medals for saving dogs anyway. People shoot them sometimes, and it's not always out of necessity. The white dog moseys around the guard post and watches us. We must look like idiots as we try to avoid the porcupine quills and swat at the flies buzzing around our helmets. Then for no reason the dog walks away, through the space between the back gate and the wall, and out along the dirt road ahead of the guard post and into the dark. Blount clicks off his moonbeam after the dog leaves. The road from the back gate leads all the way to the Green Zone, but I doubt the dog will walk that far. The Green Zone is where the Royal Marines go to fight the terrorists.

The flies scatter once the dog is gone and then a pack of jackals begins howling near the old barracks that sits abandoned along the road. I've been watching that old concrete building out there from the moment we started our shift. I figure it's an old barracks because of all the windows, and it's plain and rectangular, designed for efficiency, a place where enlisted people used to live. Blount and I had only been on post a few minutes before the barracks seemed to materialize from the shadows, as if it had not been there a moment sooner. Or at least that's how my eyes tricked me as they adjusted in the dark.

"Goddamn," Blount says after the flies clear out and the jackals' howling dies back down. "Scorpions in our house, hornets as big as crawdads, screaming jackals, and giant porcupines." Blount's a tall, goofy motherfucker, and I don't know him very well yet. Someone in the platoon told me his grandfather owns a chain of grocery stores in the South, but I haven't asked him about that. He whistles a weird catcall to himself and I know I'm supposed to tell him not to make noise on duty, but I'm distracted too. I'm just as freaked out as he is. I've never seen shit like that dog before. When I was a kid, my family took our dog to the vet to put her down. There was another dog at the clinic with quills in its muzzle, but they were small. Nothing like the ones tonight. How were we supposed to know there were giant porcupines here?

"Giant porcupines," I say. "Another thing we weren't ready for." We've been in this war almost nine years and we still don't know what we're doing. We weren't prepared for Kajaki. On our first night here earlier this week, we carried our gear to an empty house within the walls of FOB Z. The Soviets used it in the eighties and now it's our turn. We found graffiti all over the walls and scorpions skittering around on the floor. We spent the night clearing all the rooms of scorpions as if we were going door-to-door clearing out terrorist strongholds. We brushed the scorpions into a bucket and flung them over the wall in the backyard, sending them down the hill towards the river. No one will miss them. This place is crawling with bugs, overflowing with them. The next morning, Blount and Vargas found these big hornets flying laps around the house like they were practicing for an insect Indy 500. Johnson says they might not actually be hornets. Who cares if they're not hornets? I just know I don't want them crawling on me.

"What's next?" Blount says.

I look up at him and I say, "Dinosaurs," because this place feels like prehistoric times compared to our homes in the States, back in a city or in a newly built subdivision next to some cornfields like where I grew up. The whole place is after you here, not just the Taliban. If it's not some kind of poisonous bite that gets you sent down to Camp Leatherneck on a medevac, then it's the desolation of the land itself, the very ground we're on. You die if you get lost in the desert. We never had anything like this to worry about back home.

"So that's it," Blount says, and then, "Wonder what a five-five-six would do to a dinosaur."

"Probably nothing," I say. I don't really know how to imagine a dinosaur. I'm not that creative. I imagine what a five-five-six would do to a dog, and if it's worse than what the local porcupines are capable of. I didn't come to this country to worry about dogs, though. I didn't come to this country to shoot dogs either, but I definitely didn't come here to worry about them. Sorting out the reasons why I came here feels like a waste of time, even when all we have is time to waste. There's nothing to do but stand here and think about the past. I know I didn't come here to stand firewatch like this, that's for sure. No one wants firewatch.

It's so dark out it's nearly impossible for us to see anything without NVGs, even with our eyes adjusted to the dark. The Brits are watching from observation posts on the mountaintop next to the back gate. They have to be using NVGs at the OP up there, which would make the two of us obsolete down here, which would make what we're doing busy work. We're just poges, personnel other than grunts, marines who aren't infantry. So what the fuck are we doing on post to begin with? Goddamnit. I try not to yawn. I don't want to set a bad example.

Staff Sergeant Rynker, the advance party senior enlisted in charge, the higher-up who put us on the back-gate duty roster, doesn't understand that we have other shit to do, shit related to our actual MOS as landing support specialists, the shit that we trained to do in our job school, the shit we prepared to do during our pre-deployment workup exercises. I've only met Staff Sergeant Rynker in person once, and briefly, but I know enough not to like him. I try to keep myself and my marines away from him, out of sight, out of mind as they say. He came here with us as part of the advance party in order to make preparations for the arrival of the inbound US Marine artillery battery and its command element. For now, he's in charge of running base operations, so he's the type to find busy work for people who don't look busy. He wouldn't be putting our names on the duty roster if he understood or cared about what we're accountable for.

We've still got about an hour left before anyone comes to relieve us, so we stand quietly in the Helmand night and wait. You're doing good as long as you can stay awake. There's nowhere on FOB Z to get a shot of espresso before going on post at zero dark thirty, but if I wanted I could chew on the coffee grounds packaged in an MRE to stay awake. I know enough people who do that for real. I would be lying if I said I hadn't at some point, and if I said it didn't work wonders to keep me awake. It always helps if you're desperate. How could anyone fall asleep with a mouthful of coffee grounds? Fuck. I would chew on coffee tonight if I had some. Blount's the only one who has an extra MRE though. I guess if he's carrying it in his daypack right now then I could just tell him to give me the coffee grounds and maybe he would listen, but whatever.

My eyes are dry as hell. The old barracks flickers in and out of focus with each blink. I notice a window on the side of the building we're facing, but when I blink again there's only a blank wall in its place. I need more sleep, which is typical. It's practically by design that we don't get enough sleep, like some kind of unwritten rule.

"Why'd you join the Marines," I ask Blount, because you pass the time by talking about dumb shit like that, plus I haven't gotten to know him that well and you're supposed to know your marines. It's one of the leadership principles on our official list, but it's not like I had to study for a test when I got promoted. If it really is a leadership principle, it's one that most leaders don't follow very well. I guess it's on me to change it if I'm going to call out other leaders. Blount and I have been in the same platoon since I transferred during workup training, but we haven't worked at the same FOB until now.

He reflects on my question for a moment and finally says, "Army office was closed," but, he doesn't laugh. I don't know if I should take it as a joke. He could be making it up. He could be telling the truth. He might be serious. Nothing much surprises me anymore. I try my best not to laugh, but I can't help it. It's too dark to see if Blount is smiling.

"What about you, Corporal?" asks Blount. For a moment, I can't decide whether or not to tell him the truth about my brother Bryce or to make up some bullshit. I don't like thinking about my brother, let alone talking about any of that.

"College sucks," I say. "I mean, not always. But a lot of the time. Yeah." My answer doesn't begin to scratch the surface. I was only in school a couple years, and even then it's too easy to remember the good things while forgetting all the shit I hated or the experiences that made me feel terrible. But even worse than college is the Marines. I thought enlisting was an escape from all the bullshit you have to put up with in college. Waking up early, studying, dressing up for job fairs, you name it. Turns out the Marine Corps isn't a great place to go if you want to escape bullshit.

"*Don't* be cool," says Blount. "Stay *out* of school."

"Exactly," I say. Then for a while I say nothing. We wait silently except when answering the radio checks.

"Radio check, over," says a fuzzy voice through the radio speaker, calling to us from the COC, the most important building on base, where the higher-ups conduct tactical and operational planning. It's best not to be there if you don't have to be.

"You do it," I say to Blount.

"Kill," he says. He picks up the hand receiver and holds it near his face, stretching out the spiral cord connecting it to the olive drab radio. "Lima charlie, over," says Blount into the hand receiver.

"Roger, out," says the fuzzy voice, and that's it.

Eventually, a couple lance corporals from the artillery advance party walk up to relieve us and take over the guard post. We don't know either of them and I am not interested in getting to know either of them at the moment, so we don't introduce ourselves. Blount tells them to be on the lookout for big old porcupines. They look at us but neither of them answers. I know I wouldn't know what to say if someone told me some shit about porcupines. I would tell him to fuck off if I said anything at all.

We walk back to our scorpion-free house, which sits down the road from the back gate in a row of abandoned houses. There's no door on any doorframe, no glass to seal the windows. We simply walk across the open threshold at the front doorstep and then we're inside. Vargas and Johnson are sound asleep on their cots, Vargas in the front room where Blount and I sleep, Johnson in a room by himself on the other side of our house. The butt stock of Vargas's M16 lies next to his face, the rest of the rifle hidden inside his green sleeping bag. I walk out back to brush my teeth out-side, then I get undressed and climb into my own sleeping bag on the floor, but I do not bring the M16 inside the sleep-ing bag with me.

Vargas talks in his sleep. He whispers at night. I noticed it before we came here, when we were still at Delaram II. I heard him from the other side of our tent back then, and he's doing it again now, whispering from his spot in the corner. But I can't understand him. I try to keep my eyes open, despite how tired I am. There's a drawing of a boat and a stick figure on the wall next to my cot. When I close my eyes, I see the white dog looking up at us in the red light, waiting for us to do anything to help, the side of its head stuck with a cluster of the biggest porcupine quills I've ever seen. And we're just standing there watching it suffer, acting like we're not responsible for anything because we're farther from home than we've ever been.

II

Three dogs sit outside the chow hall and beg for food before breakfast. The white dog from last night is not with them. I notice Blount is inspecting the area as we walk across FOB Z, like he's also on the lookout for the dog. He breaks off from our group to peek around the corner of a building as we pass by. He shields his eyes from the sun and looks up at the OPs on the mountain. He doesn't say anything about the dog before morning chow.

We sit down at the red wooden picnic tables in the chow hall and we finish the eggs and sausage prepared for us by the Brit cook. They're not all technically British, but we call them all Brits anyway. We don't rush to finish our food even though you're always supposed to. We savor each bite. It's the best food we've had in months, better than Delaram, which wasn't bad, and even better than the sandwich shop back at Leatherneck. There's more going on in this chow hall than what we're used to. A large television sits at the front of the room with a rerun of a World Cup game playing on mute. A red bookshelf in the corner holds versions of novels like *The Da Vinci Code*, printed with different spellings of words like *tire* spelled with a *y*. The Royal Marines eat at tables around us and extend distant greetings in the form of a nod or a tip of their cups in our direction. A small group of US Marines, the advance party artillery, eat at a table alone and ignore us. We flew in on the same helicopter as them, but none of us have spoken directly to each other, not for reasons other than official business. We all wear the same uniform, but that's about it. They're combat arms, so they look down on poges like us. Their job is to get here to prepare for things like the change of command and the overall transition that takes place when the rest of their unit arrives.

When we finish eating, we meet our platoon commander at the main gate. We call her *the lieutenant* or *the ma'am* when she's not around, but we address her as *ma'am* if we address her at all. She's suited up in her flak vest with an M4 carbine slung across her back, but she's not wearing a helmet. Her Kevlar helmet hangs from a carabiner at her side. The light reflects off her tightly bound black hair as bright as if it were reflecting off the face of a wristwatch.

"Good morning, ma'am," I say as the four of us gather around.

"Good morning, Corporal," she says. She only addresses me by rank, but if she wanted to, she could use my name. She's in charge, so she sets the tone of our interactions. I think I trust her, but she doesn't trust me, that's for sure. If she did, then she wouldn't have come to Kajaki with us at all, let alone for the first couple weeks like she has planned. Whether the junior marines trust me or not, I'm still not sure. They don't know as much about my past fuckups as the lieutenant.

Back at Delaram, my platoon sergeant noticed how much time I was spending at the internet center. He did some digging online and found a blog that I had been publishing. I wasn't stupid enough to violate operational security like I was accused of, but I left my name right on the front page of the site like a moron. Anyone could have searched my name and found it. My writing disparaged some people in our command, so that was a no go. They had to punish me for that, but no one could punish me too much without making themselves look bad. I took the blog offline and the lieutenant did a page eleven on me, which goes right in your service record, but is mostly just a slap on the wrist. As far as I know, most people in the platoon still don't know about any of that.

I know the lieutenant chose me for this mission as a punishment of sorts, because of the remoteness of the location and the unlikelihood that there would be internet access here. She never had to tell me that directly, it's just obvious. There's nothing here to see or do, which means there's no danger of me writing about anything that happens. I still have my notebook and some pens, but all of the original blog entries from the notebook have been thrown out at this point. I got rid of all that to try to forget how stupid it made me feel to have my own words used against me.

Our platoon is spread so thin across the Helmand Province that the lieutenant didn't have any corporals or sergeants available for Kajaki other than me. All the other NCOs were running shifts at their own flight lines. On her end, getting stuck with me probably seems like a punishment too. I would never know if that was the case and it wouldn't be appropriate to ask her. I can't confide in anyone else either. The other NCOs in the platoon are assholes, and it's not like I can tell any of this to the junior marines in confidence. When the lieutenant told me we were coming here, she said I should be honored to lead the first team of landing support marines in Kajaki. No other red-patchers have beaten us here. We're the first ever. Now it's time to prove we belong. Our platoon is only supposed to be in-country about two more months, and hopefully the four of us will only spend one of those months in Kajaki after the lieutenant leaves. I hope this matters someday.

The lieutenant briefs me on the plan of the day while the others stand off to the side, the others being the junior marines: Lance Corporal Johnson, an African American; Lance Corporal Vargas, a Mexican American; and Lance Corporal Blount, a Texan American. What does that make me, a white guy from the Midwest, a Flyover American? It doesn't matter. None of us have worked together, and Johnson comes from HE, the heavy equipment platoon specialized in driving forklifts and loaders. HE and LS spend a lot of time working together, but none of us have worked with him yet.

The lieutenant says we're going up to the landing zone, so that's what we get ready to do. While she speaks, I nod. My sunglasses hide the fact that my eyes are distracted, not by the lieutenant, but by some mountain peaks in the distance behind her. The lieutenant may not be looking at me either. Maybe she is also looking past me at something in the distance. That could very well be since she's a big-picture person, but it's impossible to tell where she's looking with the black Oakley Gascans hiding her eyes. I don't feel bad for zoning out because there's nothing new about seeing an LZ if you've been in LS a year or more. An LZ is just a designated spot for helicopters to land. There's not much to it.

A couple Brits wearing brown T-shirts and desert-camouflage pants drive up in a small, tan open-top truck. They climb out to greet us and the driver overpronounces the word *lieutenant*, maybe to stop himself from saying *leftenant*, which is how they say it across the pond. The lieutenant introduces herself and shakes the Brit's hand. He's wearing a flak vest over his brown T-shirt and I notice a helmet sitting on the driver's seat. I recognize the rank patch on his flak vest as a sergeant, three stripes, but he doesn't introduce himself as one.

"Just call me Arnold," he says. I've never heard a sergeant in the US Marines introduce themselves by any name without the word *sergeant* preceding it. Very relaxed. He puts a helmet on his bald head and gets ready to take us outside the wire. "All right, lads?" he says to us. If I had to guess I'd say Arnold is about thirty-five, which would make him older than the sergeants I've served with in the US Marines by ten years or more. Maybe he just looks older than he is. Arnold's passenger introduces himself as Red. He's the forklift driver. He's got one chevron on the front of his vest, which makes him a lance corporal I think, the same rank as our junior marines. Our new friends are in the British Army, serving as attachments to the Royal Marines to run the LZ for them, which means they've been doing what we're about to do: spend all our time receiving and sending out cargo and passengers. It sounds simple, but things like this are always more complicated than they need to be.

"Is your real name Red?" Vargas asks as the junior enlisted introduce themselves and shake hands.

"If it's what the color sergeant calls me," says Red, taking off his helmet to reveal a head of brown hair.

"I thought your hair would be red," says Blount.

Red shrugs. He looks older too, especially for a junior enlisted. I outrank him and he looks older than me. I would hate the feeling of someone younger being a higher rank. It's the worst feeling having to kiss up to some kid. It's why no one likes lieutenants, and probably leftenants for that matter. At first glance, all the Brits look older than us, the tattooed commandos at breakfast and now these two logistics poges.

"This is Corporal Loyette," the lieutenant says to Arnold. I shake Arnold's hand while the lieutenant continues. "He'll be running the LZ after I leave. He's a good NCO." The lie is that she doesn't know if I'm a good NCO or not, considering I was only promoted a couple weeks ago. My platoon sergeant could've non-rec'd me for promotion, considering they had just filed a page eleven in my record, but for some reason he did not. The lieutenant was promoted the same day as me for that matter, from second to first lieutenant. I wonder if she was pissed when she saw me picking up rank. You don't usually get promoted right after you get in trouble.

"You have many quality months ahead of you," Arnold says to me with a smile, *months* plural. I hope he's wrong about that. I don't want to be here longer than one month, like the lieutenant told me. It better only be one month. Those soft mattresses at Delaram seem more and more like a fantasy every day. It feels like we were never there.

The lieutenant climbs into the passenger seat of the Brits' truck and I sit in back with Blount and Vargas. Johnson crams into the cab of the Brit forklift with Red. They'll be leaving it behind for us when they leave here and head down to Sangin, so Johnson needs to learn how to operate it. Arnold drives us up to the front gate. The guards open the gate and let us pass through in the truck. And then we're outside the wire under the desert sun.

Arnold steers our truck on a gravel road that snakes back and forth alongside the Helmand River. Local men employed by a private security firm stand up from their seats in the shade to open and close checkpoint gates for us. They wear gray uniform shirts and carry loaded AK-47s slung over their shoulders. They wave and smile as if they've known us for years. What are they so happy about? Vargas and Blount wave back, but I do not.

I take inventory of the new surroundings. On our first night, we landed in the dark and we couldn't see anything, just dim lights flickering through the windows of some of the local homes as we were driven from the LZ with our gear. Now we can see that the sides of the road are strewn with garbage and debris, abandoned vehicles and old shipping containers. A few cheap apartment buildings sit under trees near the riverbank. It's different than Leatherneck or Delaram, which were surrounded by desert. Everything here is green, especially the river water rushing by. Everything I've seen in this country until now has been dust. But the Helmand River is alive.

The road ascends up the side of a cliff until we reach the Kajaki Dam, an artificial structure built sixty years ago by some American engineer, but it was never finished. Arnold tells us all about it as we bounce around in the back. The dam blocks up the river to provide power to a significant portion of Afghanistan. It's a strategic point in our area of operation. We want it. The Taliban want it. It's a contested spot, but we're well protected at our current base, so they tell us. Arnold sounds like a tour guide. Our first glimpse of the dam reveals it to be a massive pile of dirt and rocks. Enormous terraces descend from the top of it down to the powerhouse on the riverbank like steps in a giant rocky staircase. It's not like any dam I've ever seen, not that I've seen many to be fair.

We turn left and we ride across the top of the dam, which serves as a bridge between the main road and the LZ. On our right is the massive lake created by damming the river, easily a mile or two across from our angle, if not greater than that to the east. Arnold pulls the truck up to an old excavator, a piece of machinery that has been abandoned for decades. The arid climate has preserved the yellow paint and prevented rust. Arnold kills the engine. He and Red remove their helmets and flaks, and they leave their SA80 rifles lying unattended across the driver's seat. But the lieutenant leaves her helmet and flak on, and she keeps hold of her M4, so I follow her lead and the junior marines follow my lead in turn. They might not want to listen to me, but they have to, just like I have to listen to the lieutenant, and she has to listen to the company commander, and the company commander has to listen to the battalion commander and so on. For now, we don't drop our gear. We are, after all, outside the wire where poges don't belong. Outside the wire is where the bad guys can get you.

Blount and Vargas walk over to a large yellow bucket attachment that's been removed from the excavator, lying on its side. Each one of them stands inside the enormous bucket, which can fit at least one adult standing up straight. I walk around with the lieutenant as Arnold shows us around the LZ, continuing his role as a tour guide. This is our domain now, or it at least will be once the Brits are all gone. It's not much to behold, but it will be ours to be accountable for and to take pride in. We have the *privilege* of facilitating the movement of passengers and cargo via helicopter. What they tell us.

The LZ here is an empty gravel lot on a plateau, the dam being the only bridge in or out. A small guardhouse sits atop a hill overlooking the area on the LZ side of the dam. The guards live there permanently. A few men sit around drinking from teacups, wearing the same uniforms as the gate guards along the road. One of them lifts his mug at me when he sees I'm looking up at them. I give a slight wave.

Arnold explains how everything functions here, where the helicopters land, where the Brits will stage their net loads in order to haul the gear out externally, everything we need to know in order to take charge of the space on our own when they leave. I jot a few things in my blue notebook, so the lieutenant thinks I'm being studious. I was not very studious in college because I didn't want to be there. Sometimes I think I could've finished two more years of college and become a lieutenant myself. If I held out a little longer. I feel like I could do what she does, manage enlisted people and fill out spreadsheets or whatever. Shit, I already do both those things for half the pay.

This all feels like a waste of time because we already know how to do this job. The only thing that concerns me is having a computer at the FOB with network access, because its 2010 and we don't use carrier pigeons anymore. I don't need a computer to write a blog. I need internet access to see the flight tracker, otherwise I won't know what the fuck's happening on a day-to-day basis. Arnold tells us there's a flight scheduled soon and we can use it as training to prepare for our job over the next month. Lucky us. The lieutenant smirks at the sound of the word *training*.

She and I talk with Arnold about the upcoming flight after we return to the FOB, basic details. The others smoke cigarettes with Red. We hash the details out with Arnold and then he parks the truck with the other vehicles and carries on with the rest of his day. The lieutenant checks in with me again. It's been a few hours of standing around outside and talking about what everyone's going to be responsible for while we're here, boring shit.

"What do you think, Corporal?" she asks. I guess she's just talking about the LZ and the setup overall. It could mean anything, and her tone makes it sound like she's putting on special gloves to talk to enlisted, like the way my father talked down to us as kids. My brother used to hate that.

"Easy shit, ma'am," I say. "We've done all this before." It's true to a certain degree, but for most people in the platoon, this is our first deployment, even for the lieutenant. We're all still learning.

"That's what I like to hear," she says. I wonder how old she is, maybe two years older than me at the most, but still an officer, a world away. I've never gotten to know an officer as a person. You can't be as honest around them in my experience. You have to play nice. So I don't tell her that I worry about running the LZ after she's gone, because it's scary. There are just the four of us with no support from our battalion, just the artillery battery we're attached to; it seems crazy. It's a real war and this ad hoc shit is the best anyone can do after all these years. But I would never say any of that to the lieutenant. I don't tell her I worry about being responsible for other people's lives. Maybe she's gotten used to that, but I haven't. Being in charge here isn't the same as back in garrison. When you're responsible for someone in garrison, Camp Lejeune, North Carolina, for instance, you make sure they get to work on time. You make sure their barracks room is clean. You make sure their uniform is squared away for inspections and they have a fresh haircut every Monday morning. All the basics. When you're responsible for someone here, you have to make sure they don't die.

III

The lieutenant dismisses us, but there's not much to do when we're not working. There's a gym set up outside with weight benches and pull-up bars, so we could get some PT in, but it's already too late in the day, too hot for that. Maybe we could spend the rest of the day watching the World Cup on the chow hall TV with the Royal Marines. They're a little intense about it though, which doesn't sound very relaxing. The other option is the bookshelf in the chow hall, I guess. But I don't feel like reading. I join the others to smoke. They've dropped their gear to hang out at the smoke pit. The smoke pit is always improvised at a place like this. The one here is a modest dirt area, surrounded by HESCO barriers. It sits on a rocky outcropping at a corner of the FOB, overlooking the abandoned marketplace across the river where the shop owners have all been driven out by the Taliban.

The old concrete barracks from last night sits outside the smoke pit in the opposite direction, perched atop a rocky hill that leads to the bank of the Helmand River below us. Piles of rusty metal and other trash blanket the ground all the way down to the riverbank as if people have been dumping garbage here for years. Shreds of plastic wave in the breeze, caught against rocks or in the branches of dead bushes. Dust everywhere.

"What's the deal with *that*?" Blount asks Red as I light a cigarette. He points at the abandoned building.

Red breathes out a cloud of smoke. "Soviet barracks from the eighties," he says. "They used to come here for R and R. Ain't that rich? Gave them a little break from the war. The Afghans owned it before them. See the pool over there?" He points off in the direction of the chow hall. There's an empty swimming pool next to it that is full of twigs and pine needles shed by the trees in the center of the FOB.

"R and R?" Blount says. "The Commies had more fun than us?"

"Everyone has more fun than us, fool," says Vargas.

"Like you didn't have fun in Kandahar," I say. But I'm only half kidding. I'd been jealous when some of the marines in our platoon spent the beginning of the deployment in Kandahar. We were eating fried chicken patties at Leatherneck filled with hidden slivers of bones while these fuckers had a TGI Fridays. That was the rumor we heard.

"No fun getting skinned alive," Red says. He laughs at our surprised reactions.

"What?" says Blount.

"That's what happened to the Soviets, mate. The ANP blokes call it *the militia house*. Some of them were muj in the eighties." His words are all it takes to get our attention. It's suddenly more than just an abandoned building now. The militia house stares back from across the way, defiantly out of place amidst the desolate natural surroundings, or fitting right in depending on how you look at it. It's just as bleak and desolate as everything else out there. But who am

I to know what's out of place here? I don't know what's normal here without a war happening.

"Don't mean to slag off Sergeant Worth," says Red. "I mean *Arnold*. But he leaves things out when he tells stories. He likes boring convoy stories, but there's more than that." We wait silently as Red finishes his cigarette, keeping us on the hook. Then he tells us the militia house is haunted.

"Bullshit," says Johnson, who pulls a digital camera from a pouch on his flak vest and begins snapping pictures of the militia house. Maybe he's got some good angles through the concertina wire coiled atop the HESCOs, even though there's not much to see. The militia house, as they call it, is just a plain two-story rectangle. There's nothing exciting about it, even if you had the best camera in the world and were the most talented photographer. It's set in the dirt with a mountain behind it, surrounded by rocks, dead bushes, and garbage.

"I'm not takin' the piss, mate," Red says to Johnson. He shakes his head and tells us the whole story. The Soviets fucked up and lost their war, then the remaining soldiers in the area were driven into the militia house, where they made a last stand with their backs against the wall, literally. The mujahideen cornered them inside and killed them all, and then skinned them according to Red's story. Or skinned them first and then killed them—Red admits he doesn't know what the order was. He says he hasn't heard the story in a while and does not tell us who he first heard it from.

"That's the legend," Red says.

"Holy shit," Blount says, and then, "Let's check it out!"

"What the fuck are you talking about?" I say. "It's outside the wire."

"But it's right *there*," Blount says.

"*Corporal*," I say. I flick my cigarette butt over the HESCOs.

"It's right there, *Corporal*," Blount says. He pleads with Vargas, who's been hanging back quietly with his hands in his pockets, forgoing the cigarettes that the rest of us have come to need about every five minutes. Vargas is usually one of the most squared away marines in the platoon, so I don't tell him to get his hands out of his pockets. I would if he was a shitbag. He glances at me and then up at Blount.

"I'd go," Vargas says. He shrugs.

"Come on, Johnson," Blount says. "Don't you want to see something cool for once?"

"Not really," Johnson says. He puts the camera away and then folds his arms.

"You don't want to go in there, mate," says Red before I can tell Blount to shut the hell up about it. "We went in once and it was all full of rubbish and shite. Dodgy place there, couldn't tell you how long I was inside."

"Dog shit?" Blount asks.

"Yes?"

"We saw this dog at the back gate last night. Looked like it got attacked."

"Attacked?" Red narrows his eyes and takes a drag on his cigarette.

"Looked like a big ass porcupine got him," Blount says. Red blows out smoke and looks at him like he's a nutcase. "Never mind," Blount says. He looks at me like I'm supposed to say something, but I don't back up his story. Besides, Red tells us, we don't want to go walking around outside the wire with all the land mines left behind by the Soviets, and he repeats that we don't want to go inside the militia house. He lights another cigarette. The militia house doesn't seem to be very interesting to him, or that's what he wants us to think. He changes the subject. He would rather talk about the movie *Zombieland*.

"Proper film," he says. "Fucking quality." Then he finishes smoking and says he's off to his barracks. "Cheers, dudes," he says, and disappears across the FOB. After that, I release the other three to do whatever they want for the rest of the day, whatever it is around here they could possibly occupy their time doing.

"Don't drink and drive; don't travel farther than two hundred miles this weekend," I say, which gets a chuckle from Vargas. Every Friday back at Camp Lejeune we'd get some stupid safety brief where an officer would tell us not to fuck up while on weekend liberty. *Make safe choices. Make smart choices. Don't be stupid.* They forced these briefs on us before every weekend began, because at least one marine in the company would inevitably have not been safe or smart by the time Monday rolled around, whether they got a speeding ticket or something worse.

The junior marines walk back to our house together and I wait at the smoke pit for a moment. I watch the militia house. It's just a quiet old barracks at first glance, a simple concrete box with divots chipped out of the walls exposing rebar beneath, evidence of years of wear and tear or possibly the damaging effects of small arms fire. But there's something else about it. I study the windows, their broken cross bars jagged like fangs in a snarling mouth. If anyone were watching me from within, they would be enshrouded in darkness and I wouldn't know they were there. The windows are like demonic eyeballs, completely black so you can't tell exactly where they're looking.

IV

Staff Sergeant Rynker puts our names on the duty roster again, even though I'm pretty sure he knows we've got an external lift scheduled in the morning and could use the sleep. But you can't argue. The lieutenant says Staff Sergeant Rynker doesn't have enough marines here yet to keep the back gate covered without us. He's like any other staff NCO, meaning that if you were to try to explain to him why you really needed sleep, he would tell you to get fucked. I make sure my name goes on the roster again, so the junior marines continue to get the most sleep, otherwise they'll complain. I know, because I would if I was in their situation. Plus, it makes me look like a good leader, like I care. I mean, I really do care, but perception is reality, as they say.

Vargas and I wake in the middle of the night and gear up while Blount snores. Vargas never questions anything or gives anyone any problems, not that I know of. And he was always cool during workups back when we were both junior marines, but I hadn't met him before then. We put on our helmets and flak jackets, and we grab our rifles before heading out the front door. We walk down the row of houses and reach the back gate, where we relieve the guards. This time I look closely at the militia house. Tonight, the clouds block out any moonlight and all I can see is its vague, rectangular shape in the dark. I want to know whether there was a window on the second deck or not, because I can't remember since standing on post last night. I don't know why it bothers me so much. I also wonder about the dog, if it will come back, and if it does, will it come from inside the house, or some other random place? Maybe it's already dead. It was in bad shape.

I don't ask Vargas about the militia house while we stand and wait. I ask him about the book he's reading. One of the Harry Potters, I don't know which one. They're all the same to me. It's a big, thick book, which makes it seem challenging and important. He's been reading it the whole deployment as far as I can tell. I think I saw him carrying it around during workups too.

"You ever gonna finish that fucking book?"

"Yes, Corporal," says Vargas. "I like to read slow."

"How'd you fit that thing in your pack anyway?" I ask. "It's as big as a damn Bible."

He laughs. "I got mad Tetris skills from logistics, Corporal. Let me know if you want me to bring a Bible next time. I could probably fit one."

"Hah," I say. "I don't think I need a Bible, but knock yourself out if that's your jam."

"Nah, I'm good."

"Oh, you don't believe in God?" I say.

"Not really."

I would never say it to him, but the real reason he's here with us is because he's not married. When the lieutenant gave me a list of marines in the platoon and said to choose two for this mission, I chose him and Blount because they aren't married, unlike a lot of other junior marines in the platoon. It's fucked up when your platoon commander tells you to pick the people going to the middle of the desert with you. Johnson is married, but I didn't choose him. According to the lieutenant, he was the only available HE operator left, otherwise we wouldn't have anyone to drive the loaders. Now he's my responsibility and I don't even know him. And all this before considering my own family. If I died here, my family would be short two sons. As much as I try not to think about Bryce, he's always in my head. I want to leave him behind, but I don't know if I can. It doesn't help that he was in the Marines too. I don't know exactly what he went through, but I'm always wondering as I have my own experiences in uniform.

"You aren't actually married, right?" I ask.

"No, Corporal," says Vargas.

"Good," I say. "Do you have any siblings?"

"My little brother. In Texas."

"Where in Texas?" I ask, as if I know anything about Texas.

"El Paso."

"Cool," I say.

When I think of El Paso I picture a desert, something that looks similar to where we are now, but with big green cactuses. I've obviously never been there. I would imagine a desert regardless of where Vargas said he was from. Blount's from Texas too, but I've never heard them talking to each other about it. No one's ever from the same place as me.

Vargas's head snaps towards the militia house and the carabiners clipped to his flak click together like car keys. I hold my M16 tight and look out towards the back road, but there's nothing there other than the shadow of the militia house. I wait for him to say something, but he stands frozen in place as if waiting for the sound of an echo. I don't hear anything and it's too dark to read the expression on his face, but I keep my voice low and ask if he's good. He doesn't answer at first.

"Did you?" he says, and then, "Never mind, Corporal."

"Did I hear anything?" I ask, trying to finish his first thought. I think of the snipers at the OPs above us. If there was anything moving around out there, they would spot it and we would hear about it over the radio. So there has to be nothing, although no one called in the dog before it found us last night. I don't hear anything near the militia house. No jackals. No wind causing the camo net on the guard post to flap around. Our radio in the guard post hisses out a garbled statement. The sound startles me and my body shudders the way it does when I wake up from a nightmare, but Vargas doesn't seem to notice.

"*COC to bravo golf, radio check, over,*" says the garbled radio voice calling from the command post, the COC. *Bravo golf* stands in for *back gate*, even though the shorthand has more syllables than if we just said, "back gate."

I pick up the hand receiver and I hold down a button with my thumb. "Lima Charlie," I say, which stands in for *loud and clear.* "Nothing to report, over."

"*Roger, out,*" says the voice, and then we're alone again until our relief arrives about a half hour later. Vargas doesn't notice when the two advance party marines show up. I have to nudge his shoulder like I'm snapping him out of a trance.

"Hey, wake up," I say. "You just zone out, or what?" Then he turns his head to me in the same startled way he had looked at the house, as if I'm evoking whatever he had seen or heard. What the fuck is wrong with him? He must need to rest up for tomorrow morning. I know I do. I wonder if there's something else I should ask him, or if there's anything I can do to help just short of telling Staff Sergeant Rynker not to put him on duty again, but that's not really my call and never will be. And I'm not a therapist, if talking to someone is what he really needs. He needs a shrink or a chaplain.

"Let's go," I say.

"Aye aye, Corporal," says Vargas. We walk back to our house and drop our gear inside. I walk out to the backyard to brush my teeth. I spit out a white glob of foam and then piss on the back wall in the dark. Vargas is in his cot and already asleep when I return to our house, facing against the corner across the room from me. He's not whispering this time, not yet. I stare at a black drawing of a ship on the wall next to our back door, a crudely rendered ship like a cruise liner with dots for portholes. The ship sits atop a jagged line that I think is meant to represent the surface of the ocean. There's a drawing of a stick person next to it with two dots and a half circle to represent its face. I look at the ship and the stick figure next to it, then Vargas starts to whisper again, but I can't understand any of it. He's too quiet. All I can hear is the faint *s* sounds, as if he's whistling some tuneless song. The sound of it is like a tablespoon of NyQuil. It knocks me right out.

V

The sun's all the way up when we get to the LZ the next day. We climb out of Arnold's truck and he escorts us over to the lot where the Brits are staging their net loads of cargo. All their gear will eventually fly south to Sangin, where the Royal Marines are headed. Some of it will get left behind when they leave, so we'll have to keep sending the rest out in small increments. Today it's our job to send out two net loads packed with rolled-up general purpose tents, the kind of fun stuff they don't put in the recruiting commercials.

"We're short on personnel for the lift," the lieutenant says to me as we wait. "We should probably have Johnson on this, just in case you need him to help out in the future."

I don't want this to be anyone's first time underneath a bird. Back home we would need someone standing underneath doing hand signals and someone standing out in front, repeating the same hand signals so the pilots could see what adjustment is needed to get the cargo hook into position. We don't need to fill those positions here though. The pilots here are experienced enough, not like the younger ones back at Lejeune. And it's the crew chief telling the pilots what to do from inside anyway; they don't really listen to us. But we still need a marine to hook up the cargo net and we'll need someone else using the static wand.

"We have someone for hookup, someone for static, and that's all we really need for this lift, ma'am," I say. I'm sure the closest Johnson has come to doing a lift is watching from the cab of a TRAM, and that doesn't need to change today. Most of the marines in our unit have never done an external lift. We've never done their jobs either, driven forklifts or anything else like that. Teaching someone how to do a *helicopter support team* isn't rocket science, but all the same I'd rather not bring someone new in when this kind of training could have been done during workups last year. That would have made too much sense.

"Johnson needs to learn eventually," says the lieutenant.

"Good to go, ma'am," I say, and then I turn to Johnson and shout, "Hey, Johnson, you're gonna learn static wand. Your job is to make sure we don't get electrocuted."

"Good to go, Corporal," Johnson says, not looking excited. If only I could tell him none of this is my choice.

"Show him how to do it," I tell Blount.

Blount takes our static wand, a yellow insulated stick with a rubber cord coiled around it, and he walks over to the forklift where Johnson and Red are smoking cigarettes. I figure the static wand is the easiest thing for someone to learn if they've never been underneath the bird before. If you've never balanced your own weight in the downwash of a helicopter, it's better not to spend your first time trying to attach the net load onto the cargo hook, which everyone calls a donkey dick because it flops around in the rotor downwash like you might imagine a horse penis doing, if that's what you're liable to imagine. The kind of shit they teach us during training. I tell Vargas he's on hookup duty, so he waits by the net load. He seems fine today. Nothing weird after last night.

As we stand around and wait for the bird, I look down at my palms, shaded brown as if I've dragged them through the moondust, bluish-gray jam packed under each fingernail. Our shower consists of a black bag that heats the water within by using the technologically advanced power of sunlight. We hang it from a wooden frame in our backyard and then open a valve to let the water flow over us while we stand naked underneath. It's no use really, so I barely bother with that. I've had athlete's foot on both of my feet for months. A pair of boots is all we're allowed to wear. The Brits are lucky as hell. They get sandals and cargo shorts issued as part of their uniform.

"Well," says the lieutenant, eyes hidden behind her black Oakleys. She finally takes her Kevlar off. Her tight regulation bun looks fake, like it could come off in one piece. She checks her watch and looks out at the LZ and perhaps beyond at the mountains.

"Everything good?" she says.

"Yes, ma'am," I say.

"Good to go."

The lieutenant nods at me. She seems pleased with everything this morning. She'll be able to tell the captain that everything here is going fine. I'm sure the CO likes hearing good news. As far as I know, the lieutenant and I have both been in the Marines the same amount of time, about two years maybe. Most everything that happens to officers is a secret to us. I heard they don't even eat with you if you're on a Navy ship together. Their lives probably suck in a different way, but if the lieutenant's not enjoying herself then she's playing it off pretty well.

"This'll be nice," says Arnold with his arms folded. "You lads can show us how it's done for a change."

"That's right," I say with a grin. "Watch and learn." Arnold laughs. He and Red are short on their deployment, even more than us. Just a couple weeks for them before it's all over and they get to go home. No one knows exactly how many days before we're on that final flight home. It's not as urgent to get us out as it was to get us in.

We wait around and chat about Arnold's career. He's been in the Army for years, was even on the first convoy to come to Kajaki, he says. It took over a week and they uncovered over a hundred IEDs along the route. None of us really know what to say to that, so we keep waiting. I only went on one convoy and it took less than twenty-four hours. I can't imagine one being longer than a week. Eventually the low thumping of a helicopter rumbles in the distance and then crescendos until two olive drab CH-47s glide out from behind a nearby hill and into the sunlight, their rotors muffled in the distance until the moment they emerge from behind the LZ guardhouse. They fly low to avoid RPGs, kicking up dust and debris. The clap of the rotors blocks out everything else, drills into our ears.

The birds do a slow circle above us. They avoid hovering directly over the guardhouse and finally settle at the opposite end of the LZ, both of their cargo ramps dropping to the gravel. Crew members in green flight suits and white helmets stumble down the ramp of each bird. Arnold waves them over to the staging area and points out the gear we're planning to send out today. The three of them all take turns yelling into each other's ear over the roar of the engines while we watch. Finally, the two loadmasters inspect the net loads, tugging on ropes and making sure the gear is secure. Everything looks good, so they walk back to one of the helicopters and disappear inside. The engines rumble as the pilots increase power.

I wave the junior marines over when the birds lift off. Johnson has the static wand clutched in both hands like a rifle. We kneel next to the cargo nets as the dust and downwash overtake us. The lieutenant hangs back, out of reach of the downwash, supervising me as I supervise everyone else. The first bird closes in. Our neck gaiters and goggles cannot save us from the sting of sand and pebbles against our faces while our arms and legs are also battered by rocks. We grab hold of the netted cargo loads to brace ourselves in the wind. The thick hose dangles from the bottom of the bird with a yellow cargo hook at the end waving around above our heads. The static electricity built up in the cargo hook would knock anyone out cold if it touched them, maybe kill them if the rumors are true. Johnson's job is to take the static wand and touch it to the hook, grounding the electric charge built up by the two rotors, which will travel through a rubber hose and into the ground. Then it'll be safe for Vargas to latch the hook onto the keeper.

The bird's rotors create dueling vortexes as it hovers. The engines blast warm air on us. I notice the white dog from our first night on post. It's watching us next to the old crane near the truck. It waits behind Arnold and Red, far enough to avoid the downwash. No one else sees it. The dog sits and waits and does not move. Then, when the cargo hook is about an arm's length from us, Johnson reaches out to secure it with his free hand before the voltage has been grounded out by the static wand in his other hand. I have to act in an instant.

I grab Johnson's wrist before it's too late and I yank him off-balance almost like I'm executing one of the MCMAP moves you learn in tan belt training. He almost falls, somehow regains his balance in the downwash, but I still feel like teaching him a lesson. I snatch the static wand and shove him again. This time he stumbles and falls to the ground. He glares through his goggles. I feel like an asshole, but he almost fucking killed himself just now. What is it that Blount didn't tell him? I wave at Blount and Johnson to get away and they both do. Then it's just Vargas and me under the bird.

I hold the static wand up in the brown dust storm and tap it against the cargo hook until I can secure the curved point around a metal cage on the side of the keeper. Even in the daylight I can see a tiny flicker of lightning jump from the hook to the wand. I grab the cargo hook with my free hand when it's safe and I hold the wand against it as it drops to about chest height, the underside of the CH-47 looming near our heads, everything around us consumed in brown. From here I can almost reach into the hellhole and high-five the loadmaster who's looking down at us from inside. He's yelling words into the mouthpiece on his helmet, directing the pilot. Vargas hooks the net load onto the cargo hook when he can finally reach. He rattles it a bit to make sure the keeper is latched securely and then he backs away. I give a thumbs-up to the loadmaster and the net legs stretch out as the bird lifts off. We make sure the legs don't get caught on anything because that's what you're supposed to do, even when there's nothing for anything to get caught on. So we wait and do nothing but keep our balance. The tents shift as the net lifts off and the first bird backs away with its new cargo as the second one moves towards us. I still feel tense with adrenaline.

I look back at Blount and Johnson. They're standing with the lieutenant, who's now supervising me from a distance. Vargas and I go through the same process with the second load, take more sand and dirt into our noses and ears. Everything goes fine with the second load. The birds rotate back in the direction they came from, and then they lurch forward and disappear behind the hill and the chopping rotor blades fade off to silence.

I look at the crane but no longer see the dog nearby. Fine. Maybe it was never there. Maybe it doesn't matter either way. I walk over to Johnson and Blount, standing off to the side with the lieutenant as if she has them under guard.

"What the hell?" I call over as I head towards him.

"I've never done this before, Corporal," Johnson says.

"Do you not know how fucking electricity works?" I ask. I hold out my open hands and say, "*Goddamn.*" Then I turn to Blount. "Did you not explain *anything* to him?"

"I mean," he says, "I thought so."

"You thought so."

He doesn't say anything else and I let out a sigh. It would be one thing if we were back at Lejeune, but here? You would think everyone would have their heads screwed on, but it's like nothing's changed from there to here. I thought getting temporary orders to deploy with this unit meant that I'd be around more experienced marines, but everyone who's an idiot in garrison is still an idiot in Afghanistan.

"All right," the lieutenant says. "Let's take the common-sense approach to this. Don't try to ground out two hundred thousand volts with our bare hands, okay? Corporal, you'll supervise and make sure everyone's properly trained for HSTs from now on."

I tell the lieutenant I won't let anything like this happen again. She's not staying here for the whole month and she'll want some peace of mind while she's back at Delaram. She'll only be here a couple more days. The junior marines listen as I reassure her. Hopefully that makes it real to them. Hopefully they can hear that I'm serious. I don't want to fuck around. I can't afford to get in trouble again, and I don't want to get anyone hurt because of me, especially not during the last two months of the deployment.

The others pile into Arnold's truck, but I want to check something before we head back to the FOB. I walk over to the old crane and do a quick lap around it, but nothing is behind it. The dog's not there, unless it's hiding somewhere nearby. I must not be getting enough sleep. Always a valid explanation. I notice something on the ground before I turn to go back. A single porcupine quill lies among the rocks, banded in white and black. It's about twelve inches long. I leave it on the ground.

VI

My watch alarm beeps at 01:45, but I lie still instead of getting up right away. I can't stop thinking about my first night on duty with Blount, the quills dug into the dog's face like something burrowing beneath its skin, the flies swarming until the dog left us alone. Now I'm lying in my cot preparing for a third round of duty at the back gate. Staff Sergeant Rynker put me on duty with Johnson, and of course it's the night after the bullshit happened during the HST, not that Staff Sergeant Rynker knows about any of that. I hate admitting to myself that the whole thing at the LZ was really my fault.

I stand up and get ready in the dark and as I'm putting my flak on I see something out of the corner of my eye. Something moves on the wall near the doorway to the backyard. I assume it's a bug at first. Maybe one of those hornets crawling around, or a spider. But it's just one of the drawings on the wall, the ship drawing I noticed the morning after we moved into our house. But now, the ship sits beneath the choppy line it originally had been floating on, making it a shipwreck. Did it really move? I wait. Nothing happens. I look away from the shipwreck and at the other graffiti, the Pashto writing and the drawings of tanks and planes. Nothing moves. I blink a few times and wait. I know I saw that ship in a different position the other day, but if I mention this to anyone, they'll just tell me I'm stressed out. Stress can make you see things you wouldn't normally see. That's what they would say. Stress can make you do things you wouldn't normally do. And they would be right. That's all it is. Stress.

I kick my boot against Johnson's cot to wake him up and I keep my eye on the wall. Nothing happens while Johnson gets ready. I have a memory as a kid of climbing out onto the wrong side of a wooden railing on the second floor of my grandmother's house. It was Thanksgiving or Christmas, some holiday when family gets together. I was maybe two or three years old, but I remember it so clearly it could have happened yesterday. As I held on and shuffled out along the railing, the stairs leading down gradually dropped off next to me until I must have been at least ten feet from the first floor. But when I let go of the railing, I didn't fall violently. In my memory, I take my hands off the railing and I sink to the floor as if someone has cradled me in their arms, carried me safely down, and set me on my feet. When I mentioned this memory to my parents later, they told me it must have been a dream. But the memory is so clear, as clear as my recent memory of the ship drawing on the wall, floating on the waterline. I wonder how often my mind makes up memories and I don't even realize it.

Johnson and I don't say anything after we relieve the off-going guards at the back gate. We just want to get the shift over with. The offgoing guards leave and we take our turn standing there. The moonlight finally reveals the side of the militia house facing us. I now see there are no windows on the second deck. I guess I could have just walked over any afternoon and looked during the day, but that never occurred to me until now. Am I always the smartest? Not really.

Nothing else happens while we're on post. The jackals howl on and off throughout our shift. Helicopter rotors beat against the sky in the distance. I'm still thinking about that time at my grandmother's house, the way my body lowered from the second floor to the first. The memory is real in my head but what's being remembered couldn't have happened. It's a real memory of a fake thing, a false event. Johnson clears his throat. He drinks from the hose on his CamelBak. I don't mention anything about the HST or anything else. Nothing was Johnson's fault, but everything that needs to be said has already been said. Eventually the next pair of guards shows up and we walk back to our house without a word.

Johnson drops his gear and falls asleep right away. As I reach into my daypack to get my toothbrush, I see that the graffiti drawing on the wall has not moved from its spot beneath the ocean's surface. Nothing has changed since the last time I looked at it. So I tell myself the jagged line was meant to be the underside of the clouds hovering above the ship, not the surface of an ocean. That makes sense. Of course the ship never moved. How could it have? It has always been where it is now, just like the stick figure next to it.

VII

The stick figure drawing is different the next morning. Lines of hair point out in random directions from its circle head, the same as before. It holds a small airplane at the end of its stick arm, which is also nothing new. But there had been a face before. There were two dots and a smiling mouth. The face is blank now. Someone must have erased it. Something feels weird. Even without either of the eyes I get this feeling like the figure is looking back at me from the wall, watching me. Any of the junior marines could have changed the drawing, for no reason other than boredom. I wouldn't put it past any of them, although Johnson doesn't seem like the type to do childish shit like that. None of them would have known that I had seen the stick figure in the first place because I never said anything about it. I never pointed it out to them or mentioned it. They wouldn't know to expect any reaction from me by changing its face. So if it was one of them, they're not doing it to fuck with me. But if it wasn't one of them, then what the hell?

I pull the edge of my sleeping bag up past my nose, just

far enough so I can still see the drawing, but hiding myself from view like those nights in my bedroom when I was a kid, lying still with a light on while staring at the darkness inside my half-open closet door. Back then I thought whatever might be inside my closet wouldn't know I was there if I didn't move a muscle. I can't shake the feeling of eyes on me. I stare at the drawing. I wait until the others wake up before I move, and then we walk to morning chow together and I wonder if I'm going crazy.

After we're done, I tell the lieutenant I'm taking the junior marines over to the Royal Marines' gym so we can get some PT in. The Brits are out on patrol, so we're free to use their workout gear. They have a few weight benches set up under a camo net, but I've noticed a pull-up bar off to the side as well, and if the Marine Corps has taught me anything it's that pull-ups are the most important exercise of all. You always have to be good at pull-ups. The junior marines aren't as optimistic about pull-ups as I am when I tell them to drop their blouses and follow me to the gym. No one appreciates the idea.

"I'm good," I hear Johnson say from his bedroom in the back of our house. He likes to lounge on his cot and watch movies on his laptop. I mean, any of us would be doing that if we had our own laptops. On one hand I want to let him stay here and do whatever he wants. Eventually the battery will die. Then he'll have nothing else to do until the rest of the artillery battery flies in, hopefully with some power adapters. We can't plug any of our electronics into the outlets here.

"Let's go," I say. "It's not a request. You're one of us as long as we're here, and this is what we're doing." Eventually, when we're done with our job here, Johnson will go back to the HE platoon, but we haven't reached that point yet. He finally comes out of his room wearing a pair of Oakleys.

"Aye aye, Corporal," he says.

We carry our rifles with us and stack them together to keep the barrels from touching the ground. There's a pull-up bar with some ragged tape wrapped around it, and two lower rusty horizontal bars running parallel to each other. I make the junior marines complete three circuits of a max set of pull-ups, twenty push-ups, fifty crunches, and ten dips. The camo net only blocks some of the sun and the whole routine turns out to be hell right away. I've stayed in shape throughout the deployment and I thought up this particular circuit knowing I could complete it myself, but even I wonder if I can complete three full sets in the heat. Blount freaks out, sweat beading up on his red face.

"We shouldn't even fucking be here," he says to himself while waiting in line for Johnson to finish his pull-ups.

"Excuse me?" I say.

"I mean in Afghanistan, Corporal."

Johnson drops from the pull-up bar and laughs at Blount. At first he looks like he's going to say something, but then he just shakes his head and walks away. I don't know what to say, so I shrug. I haven't been thinking about any of that lately. I've been thinking about other things, like athlete's foot. Blooms of itchiness flare out from between my toes as we work out in the heat.

"Why shouldn't we be here, fool?" Vargas asks when no one answers Blount.

"Dude," says Blount. "We should've bombed these mofos ten years ago. We aren't back-to-back world war champs 'cause we tried to make friends with everyone. We blew all their shit up. And that was Europe. They got like, nice shit there, you know? Like gold. Or old paintings. It's just a desert here."

"Quit stalling and do your pull-ups," I say.

"This isn't World War Two, bruh," Johnson says after finishing twenty push-ups. "It's NATO and insurgents. Get on Wikipedia." It's as many words as I've heard him say in one complete sentence.

"Man, same difference," Blount says while dangling from the pull-up bar.

"Not really."

"Whaddya mean not really? You're the Black guy so you get an opinion but I don't?"

"What?" says Johnson. "What does that have to do with literally anything?"

"Hey," I say. "Don't call him the Black guy."

"Good to go, Corporal," says Blount, and then, "But if we bombed everyone it would just be a matter of time before this was over. Osama's still running around the caves and we're sitting around waiting."

"We're not sitting around, we're PTing," I say. Maybe Blount's right and we should've bombed everyone long ago. What difference would it make to anyone back home? I do fifteen pull-ups, coming to a dead hang before bringing my chin over the bar each time. The torn-up tape doesn't do much to protect my hands from the rusty, jagged metal.

"What would you do differently than General McChrystal?" I ask.

"General McChrystal?" Blount asks.

"The ISAF commander," says Johnson. Blount looks back at Johnson and blinks, then Johnson says, *ISAF, bruh.* When Blount doesn't react to that either, Johnson says, *"We're* in ISAF. *Get on Wikipedia."*

Blount thinks he knows everything, but they don't really teach you much about the big picture during workup training. For instance, we never really learned about the people here, not really. That's not something we need to know to be able to do our jobs. We hardly know anything. And we never really learned why we're still here after so many years, like why *haven't* we gotten Osama yet? No one has ever answered for that, because answering for that doesn't change things from our perspective. Our job is to do what we're told. No one brought us here to think or learn.

"Anyway," Blount says. "To answer your question, Corporal: I don't know. All's I know is we got enough bombs but we're trying to be nice to everyone. What good does that do unless our plan is to be here forever? And if we're trying to make friends, then what are all the bombs for?" Blount has a hard time with the workout because of his lanky body. It's more difficult for him to do the pull-ups, push-ups, and dips. And his long torso doesn't make the crunches any easier. He's just getting frustrated at everything else because of that.

"You're just getting frustrated because you're out of shape," I say.

"We're trying to help these people, not blow up their houses," Vargas says. The exercises are easier for Vargas with his stout frame. It's like he barely has to move when he does his crunches.

"Yeah, well a firefighter doesn't go into a building that's on fire and make friends with the people they're trying to save," says Blount. "They grab their asses and save 'em."

"Why are you so obsessed with making friends?" says Vargas. "No one wants to be friends with you." Johnson and I both laugh, but my laugh fades when I see the dog from the back gate, up on the hill behind the officers' house. The dog watches us and then turns away and disappears around a corner. Of course there are other dogs here that look similar, so maybe it wasn't the same one.

"Just kidding, fool," says Vargas. "I'll be your friend."

"Did you just see that, Corporal?" Blount asks, ignoring Vargas. He gestures towards the officers' house.

"No," I say.

"See what?" asks Johnson, so Blount tells him and Vargas about the dog at the back gate as we finish up our circuits.

"Damn," Vargas says at the end of Blount's story. "That's whack."

"It's f'd up, right?" says Blount, then he looks at me. "We should go check out the militia house before the command element shows up." I think about how easy and quick it would be if we did go. As long as we get Arnold and Red to escort us out the back gate, we should be fine, assuming the lieutenant doesn't find out. The Brits are still running the FOB, so they're in charge, and the militia house is close enough to the back gate. Nothing would happen if we're not gone long, if all we do is walk over there and have a look around. And shit, maybe there is something worth seeing in the militia house. If we don't take this chance and go now, I'll spend the rest of the deployment wondering what we would have found if we did.

"No promises, but we'll see," I say, trying to keep my tone neutral.

We walk back to our house after finishing up, and I do my best to take a shower. Our shower doesn't really do much, but it's better than nothing. I dry off with a dirty towel and then walk to the smoke pit by myself and I look at the militia house. I wonder if it's full of graffiti inside just like our house. Before I go to sleep that night, I check on the stick figure drawing and the ship. Nothing about either of them has changed since I last looked.

VIII

The next morning I ask the Brits if they'll take us to the militia house. Arnold and Red are sitting across from us at the chow hall. We've only exchanged small talk since we sat down. Arnold sets his fork on his plate when I mention the militia house, and the others stop eating and listen.

"You're telling stories again, aren't you?" Arnold says to Red, who doesn't look up from his food.

"Only true ones," Red says with a shrug.

Arnold sighs, looks across the table at me with a furrowed brow, and asks why we would want to go to the militia house. "There's nothing in there but rubbish," he says, his cheerful demeanor up to this point finally interrupted by the mention of this. Is the militia house a big deal or not?

"I guess we just want something to take pictures of," I say, figuring there's no reason to lie about it. That's all we're really doing, just looking around. It's not like we're asking to go on a field trip to a hot zone. We just want to see some cool shit to make the other marines in LS platoon jealous the next time we share stories about what we've seen. We want some easy souvenirs. Arnold looks up at the ceiling and thinks about it. I wonder how many times he's been in the militia house.

"Is there something else we need to know?" I ask.

"If it's just souvenirs, you won't find much there," Arnold says. "What about your leftenant?"

"She's got other stuff going on," I say, which is probably true, even if I never know what she's doing when she's not with us. "She'll be fine without knowing."

"Fine without knowing," repeats Arnold. "As long as you're quick about it."

We agree that the best time of day to sneak over is today, later in the morning. We walk back to our house and wait around anxiously. When the time comes, Johnson puts a digital camera in one of his grenade pouches. He's the only one with a camera. Vargas and Blount bring their daypacks in case they find anything to carry back, within reason I remind them. I tell everyone to keep their weapons unloaded for now. We're going outside the wire, but only a stone's throw from the back gate.

"What if we need to shoot someone, Corporal?" Blount asks.

"We won't need to shoot anyone," Johnson says.

"What about the lieutenant, like Arnold said?" Blount asks while clipping the chin strap of his Kevlar. If I'm already on her shit list for the blog posts, then this isn't a great way to get myself taken off. But I know she won't catch us because no one would have a reason to tell her anything. The guards on back-gate duty don't know her. They probably don't even know she's in charge of us.

"She won't know unless someone tells her," I say. "And no one's going to do that." The lieutenant will be gone tomorrow anyway. She's flying back to Delaram to oversee the platoon's operations from the company office. I gather the others when it's time and we leave our house and walk to the back gate.

"Fifteen mikes," I say. Twenty minutes seems safe, but I know they won't move fast enough if I say twenty minutes and Arnold is not eager to wait around for us to take our sweet time. In a fifteen-minute window I'm hoping we don't get a call on the PRC-117 we keep in our house. If we get a call on the radio and we don't get back in time to answer, I guess we can just lie and tell them the radio battery was dead. Worst-case scenario. Half the time it's true anyway.

I X

Arnold tells the back-gate guards what we're doing and neither of them questions him or asks us anything. Then, one at a time, we slide sideways through the opening in the gate and we find ourselves outside the wire. It's not technically my first time going outside the wire. I've spent the whole deployment working flight lines or sitting in the operations office, but I was unlucky enough to go on convoy a few months ago where I had to sit in a truck for about nineteen hours. But it didn't turn out to be dangerous. Now that we're out here there's a sudden awareness of every little detail, a sense of paranoid dread. The shadow cast by a small pebble, a tiny piece of trash blowing across the ground, a larger piece of trash set in the dirt that could be a harmless chunk of metal or perhaps a Soviet mine left over from decades ago. Every little sound is projected, a rock tumbling down a hill for instance, or a plastic bag blowing across the ground. There could be a person hiding behind anything out here. I look down at the river as we walk towards the house and I notice what appears to be old rusted hubcaps scattered along the ground. They're everywhere, mixed in with litter all the way down to the riverbank.

"Are those mines, Corporal?" Vargas asks as we file along the dirt road in the sunlight.

"They have to be," I say. I hear the clicking of Johnson's digital camera behind me. I keep reminding myself about the Royal Marines watching us from the OPs above. They would see us walking along the road if they looked straight down, but hopefully they're not paying attention. For our purposes, it would be better if they weren't. The fewer people watching us as we sneak around, the less chance word would get back to the COC and back to the lieutenant that we were gone. We'll be hidden from the OPs once we're inside the militia house anyway. Then no one will know where we are.

X

We reach the doorway and we wait outside. We can't see anything yet because our eyes are still adjusted to the sunlight, and even with sunglasses on it's too dark to see anything inside. We hear a dull moan caused by wind sweeping across the windows. Johnson and Vargas exchange silent glances through their Oakleys. I unclip the moonbeam from my flak vest and I catch a whiff of something putrid drifting out. It smells like Red was telling the truth when he said the place was all full of shit.

"We'll be waiting out here, lads," Arnold says, nodding his head towards Red and brandishing his SA80 with a magazine inserted, which feels ominous. Arnold is like a completely different person to me with a loaded weapon. It gives him an edge that feels less than inviting, like he's just as prepared to shoot any of us as he is the Taliban if they suddenly show up. "Don't be long," he says. I had hoped they would come inside, but they both refused when I asked if they wanted to join us.

Red produces a crumpled cigarette pack from a grenade

pouch on his flak and pulls out a bent cigarette. He lights it while his rifle hangs at his side and he looks at the upper floor of the building.

"Fifteen mikes," I remind everyone. Then we go in.

XI

The doorway swallows us whole and we find ourselves in a narrow hallway, standing on a filthy concrete floor. Sunlight bleeds out through a row of open rooms to reveal garbage scattered all over. We find torn-up pieces of cardboard and shredded plastic wrappers when our eyes adjust to the low light. It all looks like MRE trash. There's as much dirt and animal shit on the floor as there is human debris, unless the garbage has been gathered by animals to build nests or something. I don't know. I try breathing through my mouth but that doesn't block the smell completely. Blount groans and squeezes his nostrils between his thumb and forefinger.

"Smells like fuckin' cat piss," he says.

"Worse than that," says Johnson.

"It is what it is," I say. Scuffs and blemishes cover the walls and the ceiling, black marks and scratches, more Pashto graffiti and drawings similar to what we've got inside our house, maybe even the same artist at work here. There are a few jagged stick figures that look like close relatives of the drawing near my cot. I pan my light along the wall and find a stairwell behind us that leads up to the second deck, and another set leading down to a basement. Must be some type of bunker down there, maybe a bomb shelter, I think. Arnold would know.

"*Hello*," Blount calls to the empty hallway. He holds a hand up to his ear theatrically, but his greeting goes unanswered, not even an echo. Vargas provides his own mock echo and laughs. Blount doesn't seem to notice though. Vargas gives Blount a light punch on the shoulder to snap him out of it.

"Which way should we go?" I ask.

"Where did they skin the Russians?" says Blount.

"Nobody got skinned," Johnson says. "That's the bullshit-test story I've ever heard." He slings his rifle and unclips a grenade pouch to get his camera out. He points the camera up the stairs and snaps a picture, setting off the flash, which lights up a line of bullet holes punched into the wall. The holes trail along the wall like dotted lines on a treasure map, leading up to the second deck. Looks like someone emptied a full magazine all at once.

"Holy shit," Johnson whispers, the camera frozen in his hands. So that's it, something definitely went down here. I guess until now I've only seen the militia house as some kind of diversion from the boredom we face on the daily. I hadn't believed anything really happened here until now. I just wanted to come for the hell of it, because we could. We were all bored and nothing was stopping us, but now I feel something drawing me inside, pulling me closer. Vargas and Blount switch on their moonbeams and Johnson sets off his camera flash a few more times in the ruined stairwell. The blinks of light reveal quick glimpses of the entire tableau. Bullet holes pockmark the wall as if weapons had been fired randomly in every direction. Blount suggests we follow the bullet holes upstairs, and I'm just as curious about whatever could be waiting for us, so we go up.

XII

My watch reads 10:07. Johnson's camera flash blinks as we climb the staircase and I think about telling him to knock it off with all the damn flashing, but it's not like he'll have another chance to take pictures in here. We're not coming back, that's for sure. The second-deck hallway is identical to the first, filthy and lined with doorways. The militia house is just a typical barracks designed for efficiency. Pack as many enlisted people in here as possible.

There's just as much garbage upstairs. We split up to search the empty rooms for whatever it is we came here to find. I walk down the hall and watch my shadow as it stretches along the floors of the sunlit barracks rooms. The shadow keeps in step as if another person is walking alongside me. I choose one of the rooms at random and stop to poke my head in. There's nothing really unique about this one, not that I notice at first. It's just an empty room like the others. There's no furniture left behind from whenever the place was occupied. Everything has been removed other than whatever the animals bring in here with them. I walk inside and take a closer look at some trash in the corner.

There's a pile of clutter in the shadows, which I first take to be a bunch of sticks or a big bird's nest or something, but it turns out to be a pile of porcupine quills, like the ones from the back gate. I pick up a single quill from the tangled heap, careful not to stick myself on the ones that are pointed straight out at me like a jagged warning signal. I hold it away from my face. Who knows what kind of bacteria these things are covered with. I let the needle rest across my open hand. The end of it extends past my middle finger from the base of my palm. Holy shit. You would never want to piss off one of these things. Do I want to take this thing back with me as a souvenir, wash it off and keep it somewhere safe so it won't stab me by accident or get broken or crushed before I bring it home? I don't know if it's worth it. Either way, the sight of the quill in my hand is a great photo op for a size comparison, so I take it with me as I leave the room to look for Johnson and his camera.

XIII

Johnson's camera flash bursts through one of the doorways at the opposite end of the hallway. I glance at the graffiti and smudged writing on the wall as I walk towards the room, all written in a language I can't read. There's not enough light to see the drawings clearly. They could be drawings of anything.

I find the others gathered in the same room, which is unexpected. I thought they would split up, but they stayed together. A shroud of peacefulness envelops me when I walk into the room with them. I can't place the exact feeling. It's like an enclosure of invisible safety surrounding me, touching my skin. I've never felt this before. At first, I don't see anything remarkable about this room in comparison to the other rooms, but this one feels different, inviting, like I could stay in this room for a while and everything would be fine if I did. There's no reason to rush back to the FOB. There's nothing to look forward to back there but missions and uniform regulations and grooming standards. No one to talk to. No phones to call home. No mail. No internet.

I'm not in a hurry, but I check my watch anyway. The

time reads 10:12. Blount tells me this must be where they killed the Russians. He says he's sure of it. Johnson doesn't disagree with him. I turn my head and see the floors and the walls are charred black, burned. Then the room's full of flies, as if the bodies are still rotting in here, but I don't smell anything rotten other than the general stench of the whole building. There's garbage piled all over just like everywhere else and I see more porcupine quills scattered around. Vargas sees I'm holding one, so he kneels over a pile and picks one up to inspect it. He puts one in his pack to save for later. Blount stares up at something behind me. I turn around to see a group of bullet holes around the doorway, clustered together like wax cells in a honeycomb. This is where they made their last stand, I think. Everyone must have been shooting together. I imagine the room fogged up with smoke from AK fire. Looks like Red's little story is true after all.

I sit down and lean against a wall and swat flies from my face while studying the grim appearance of the room. Johnson takes pictures of every square inch of the space like a detective mapping a crime scene. He's taking multiple pictures of the same thing, as if he's forgetting to move on, hypnotized. Blount's daypack is lying on the floor. I remember he has an MRE inside his daypack and I feel hungry even though it hasn't been that long since we ate breakfast.

"Take that MRE out," I say. "We should eat something." There's plenty of calories in an MRE for more than one person. Plenty to share.

"Aye aye, Corporal," Blount says. He doesn't question it. No one does. They sit down on the floor with me, the flies buzzing around our heads. The camera flash blinks in our faces. Blount reaches into his pack and I see he's got the best of all MREs: menu number nine, beef stew. Everyone knows beef stew is the best MRE because it always has M&M's. The best MREs have the best candy.

"Let me get the M&M's," I say. Blount doesn't argue with me. Something in the air closes in tight against the surface of my skin like an invisible pillowcase. I wonder if I'm breathing something other than air. There's pressure against my body pushing in from the outside. Something is taking hold, pulling us in. We're fading away, but we don't want to leave. The flies continue to gather.

XIV

Blount is the first to smell it, whatever is inside the MRE. He uses both hands to rip open the package, and then chokes and flings it across the room. The partially opened MRE lands in the corner and something wet splashes out, but it falls behind a pile of trash and suddenly there are too many flies buzzing around it to see what it is. I cough and gag when the smell reaches me. My nose runs over my lips and tears spill from my eyes. There's a moist warmth radiating from the source of the rotting smell that makes the air humid and constrictive. The air reaches up through my nostrils and tugs at the back of my eyes. It drips down my throat like water. There are now enough flies in the room to dull the sunlight.

The buzzing is all I hear. They land on my head and tip-toe at the corners of my mouth and they force their way into my nose and ears. Then there's something else, lower and deeper. Maybe not a sound, but something like a pulse resonating from the floor, up through my boots, grabbing hold and squeezing the inside of me with the rhythm of a heartbeat, but out of sync with my own heartbeat. I lean forward and vomit on the floor between my outstretched legs. Some of the vomit splatters onto my desert trousers, but they're so dirty anyway no one will notice, then I hack until a hand grabs my shoulder and pulls me towards the door. There's a voice outside. It's Arnold calling to us, but he sounds a mile away.

It's taking us longer to walk the length of the second deck hallway on our way out than it did on our way in, but we're not moving any slower than we were before. The hallway stretches out in front of us as we stumble along, doubling in length. I'm on the verge of throwing up again. Someone's pulling me along, maybe Blount. As we get closer to the stairs, I see the walls rippling as if made of liquid. The graffiti appears to be floating on the surface, the drawings and the scribbles of writing bobbing up and down. I don't see much more before we run down the stairs. Nothing makes any sense. I feel like we've run four hundred meters by the time we make it to the end of the hallway and back down to the first deck. As I'm pulled outside, I notice there is no longer another set of stairs leading down to a basement.

XV

We stumble outside gasping for air as if we had been drowning in the house. Arnold and Red exchange a look but they don't seem too worried about us. In fact, they look confused and kind of irritated as we catch our breath. They ask what took us so long. The time on my watch reads 10:51, but that can't be. That makes no sense. We were inside for maybe ten minutes, that's all.

"Blokes look off-color," says Red.

"It's nearly eleven, mates," says Arnold.

"That's impossible," I say, my throat burning.

"I'll tell you what's impossible," says Blount between breaths, but I hold up my hand to cut him off.

"Enough," I say, not wanting everyone to get hysterical. I don't know how I can convince myself that nothing happened inside the militia house, let alone convince the others. Something's definitely going on, but I don't want to hear anything else about it. What the fuck happened with Blount's MRE? The image is blurry, but I can picture the torn-up package lying in the corner of the room. I don't know what I saw. I can't make sense of it. The more I think about it, the farther away it feels. I don't want Arnold and Red to think we're crazy. But I think there might be more to their story. I don't think they've told us everything.

The guards ask us if we saw anything cool as we walk through the back gate on our way into the FOB. We tell them there was nothing to see. Arnold and Red don't say anything; they treat us like we're contagious. They leave without asking about what happened. When they're gone I realize I forgot to ask Arnold about the basement, if it exists. Maybe he's been down there. The rest of us are silent as we go back to our house and drop our gear.

XVI

We go to the chow hall at lunchtime, but they give us MREs instead of real food like we've gotten used to. All the kitchen gear is packed since the Brit cook is flying out with the lieutenant's group tomorrow. I highly doubt they'll send us a gourmet chef to replace him. Now we'll be eating MREs. We've had our last real meal for the foreseeable future. I wish we would've known at the time so I could have cherished it. We stare down at our MREs as we sit at the picnic tables. I take both hands and grip the corners to open it. Blount cringes and leans away from me.

"What," I say. Everyone is focused on my hands, so no one sees how nervous I really am. I hold my breath and I tear open the MRE. Nothing happens. Nothing jumps out at me from inside and there's no smell. The others sigh together as if a bomb has been disarmed. I look inside the package. Everything seems to be normal. Blount opens his MRE when everything appears to be safe. Beads of sweat gather at his hairline. He looks pale.

"Make sure you're drinking water," I say, as if that's what will fix it. I don't want to acknowledge anything about today.

I would be admitting that we did something we were not supposed to be doing, or worse, that there's really something going on with the militia house.

Vargas looks down at the table. He shakes his head and laughs to himself after he opens his MRE, but no one adds anything else. Blount and Johnson seem a little freaked out, but I can't tell with Vargas. Maybe he's just someone who doesn't freak out easily. I don't know.

No one finishes a whole MRE. We stuff the leftovers in our cargo pockets for later, the smaller items like peanut butter packets or crackers. Blount asks everyone for their extra unwanted Tabasco sauce bottles. He's building a collection for some reason. I can't imagine what kind of scheme he's working on.

"Did you take any pictures of the basement stairs," I ask Johnson as we walk back to our house.

"Hmm," Johnson says. "I don't remember, Corporal."

"You don't remember taking a picture or you don't remember seeing the stairs?"

"Either."

When we get back to our house, Vargas lies on his cot with one boot crossed over the other as he reads Harry Potter, but after a few minutes he closes his book and stares at the ceiling. Blount tries to take a nap, but flies keep landing on his face. It's too hot to sleep under a poncho liner today. You'd be sweating out of your ears in no time. Blount doesn't read books and his iPod battery is dead, so he doesn't have anything else to do but try to fall asleep. We don't have any power adapters yet, so until then I guess we're fucked if we need any power. Things are worked out conveniently so that we don't technically *need* any power for personal electronic devices. All we *need* is secure internet access, which we have at the COC, and a green logbook, which we keep sitting on a concrete pedestal in the room where Blount and Vargas and I sleep so we always know where it is.

Vargas rolls over as I walk out through the back door. He reaches into his daypack and pulls out the porcupine quill he took from the militia house. Then he turns it over in his hands for a while, examining it. I realize I had planned to take one out with me, but I didn't follow through on that. I must have dropped it as we ran out together.

I find Johnson outside smoking a cigarette and I ask him to show me the pictures he took inside the militia house. He sighs like that's too much to ask, but he gets the camera from the grenade pouch on his flak. He turns it on and taps his thumb against the touch screen viewfinder. I wait for him to find the picture of the stairs, but all of the files seem to be corrupt. There aren't any pictures of the militia house saved that we can find. All of the images on Johnson's SD card display a black frame and nothing else.

"Fuckin' serious?" Johnson says. He scrolls through his saved photos, but all of them are now blank, even the pictures he took before we came to Kajaki. He groans. "Oh, you gotta be fucking kidding me, man." Every picture Johnson has taken in Afghanistan has been lost. Months of memories. He takes a slow breath in and out. I haven't been taking pictures in-country, but I know I'd be pissed to lose every deployment picture if I had planned to share them with people back home. Johnson navigates through camera menus until he's back where he started. He holds the camera up and snaps a shot of the back wall for the hell of it. He shakes his head upon seeing that the picture has turned out fine.

XVII

We waste time for a while before the lieutenant calls our house on the radio. I answer and she says I need to meet her at the COC. She's about to hem me up if she found out we went outside the wire. What else could it be? I would deserve whatever punishment they wanted to give me. Blount and Vargas are goofing off in the backyard, using empty water bottles like baseball bats in order to swat hornets out of the air. Johnson is alone in his solitary bedroom. I don't want anyone asking me where I'm going, so I get the blue notebook out of my daypack and I walk over to the COC without anyone noticing I've left. You have to be ready to take notes if someone gives you complicated orders because no one ever gives you anything in writing. The lieutenant is waiting for me in the front room when I reach the COC building.

"Corporal Loyette," she says from the other end of the room, standing with her hands on her hips.

"Good afternoon, ma'am," I say, bracing myself for the worst, a punishment for leaving the FOB without permission. I can't read her expression.

"I need you to fill these out so we can get you set up with SIPR access." The lieutenant picks up a stack of papers from a shelf and sets it on a table near one of the SIPR laptops. I breathe a sigh of relief and she pauses before handing me a pen to complete some paperwork. That was a close one, I think. That could have been bad, but instead I'll be able to access the flight tracker after today without having to use someone else's login info. The lieutenant doesn't seem to notice anything off about me when I show up even though I still feel sick. I have an upset stomach and a headache.

Staff Sergeant Rynker helps us enter everything into the system properly. He's a stubby man with a shaved head and wiry hair poking out the neck of his skivvy shirt. He's old and crusty, like he's been a staff sergeant for a long time, and he's the acting senior enlisted of the advance party until the rest of the battery shows up with their captain and first sergeant. I don't really get where he falls in line in with the lieutenant, who technically outranks him even though she's not in his chain of command. The lieutenant is in charge of her platoon, and she answers to our company commander, a captain, who answers to our battalion commander, a lieutenant colonel. Most of us have only seen the battalion commander in person a couple times. But Staff Sergeant Rynker doesn't answer to the lieutenant. He answers to his first sergeant, who answers to his battery commander. That's all between Staff Sergeant Rynker and the lieutenant though. Not my problem.

"Do you have any questions about anything at all?" asks the lieutenant after we've finally finished going line by line through all the forms. I notice Staff Sergeant Rynker looking over her shoulder at me, squinting his eyes as if straining to see something more clearly. He might outrank me, but he's not in charge of us when the lieutenant's around.

"No, ma'am," I say. "I'm good to go."

"Kill," she says with approval, and then, "We should've set everyone up with accounts sooner." She's right about that, but I don't say anything. She tells me to continue carrying out the plan of the day, which I take to mean *go away*.

The lieutenant walks into one of the side rooms in the COC and I turn to leave, but Staff Sergeant Rynker taps me on the shoulder, so I spin back around to face him. I keep one of my hands on the barrel of my shoulder-slung M16 and I put my other hand behind my back because talking to superiors with your hands behind your back is a sign of respect. Staff Sergeant Rynker may not be in our direct chain of command, but we still have to respect him and do what he says. He looks me over with his eyes narrowed and his arms folded, a clipboard held in one of his hands. I wait for him to ask about the militia house, to accuse me of something, but he stares at me for a whole minute before speaking.

"When's the last time you got a haircut?" he says.

"I don't know, Staff Sergeant," I say, relieved that all he's concerned with is a haircut.

"The next one is gonna be today, check?"

"Good to go, Staff Sergeant," I say.

"These damn Brits are real lackadaisical sometimes," says Staff Sergeant Rynker, scribbling something on his clipboard, glancing over his shoulder to make sure none of the Brits are listening. "They follow different rules. Time to rein that trash in, got it?"

"Yes, Staff Sergeant," I say, but I don't think anyone's haircut has ever stopped them from getting their job done. I've noticed the Brits are more lax with their grooming standards, but they don't seem to be slacking when it comes to their jobs. Staff Sergeant Rynker stares at me for another minute with his eyes narrowed as if he's trying to look right through me.

"Go down the hallway behind me," he finally says, his face downturned to emphasize a threatening glare. "Third door on the left; it's a closet. Inside the closet on the second shelf, you will find a shoebox. Inside that shoebox you will find some clippers, which you will use to trim your nasty hair. You and your marines. I see y'all's mop tops every damn day, lookin' like a straight bag of ass. You understand me?"

"Yes, Staff Sergeant," I say.

"Good," he says. "Now go away." He unfolds his arms and then fans out the fingers on his right hand as if he's physically pushing me away with the explosive gesture. He watches as I follow his instructions on where to find the clippers. The shoebox is exactly in the spot he told me it would be. If he's worried about our appearance, then that must mean the rest of the artillery battery is arriving soon. Some officers and senior enlisted must be on the way or he probably wouldn't care as much.

I carry the shoebox over to our house and I tell everyone the word: we're getting haircuts. The others are not excited. So far I've only done a good job of sharing bad news. I ask Vargas if he'll do us the honor since he's been giving us barracks cuts for five dollars a head throughout the deployment. There isn't any disbursing office to withdraw cash here, so he'll have to put us on his list. He marks us down on a folded-up sheet of paper if we don't have the cash on hand. We lean our M16s against a tree near the COC, right by the power outlet on the wall. Vargas doesn't waste any time. He gets to work on Blount while Johnson sits against the building and swats flies away from his face. I sit under the nearby tree in the shade. Blount winces after a couple minutes and jerks his head away from Vargas's clippers.

"Ow, dude," Blount says. Vargas switches off the power and taps his fingers against the hot clipper blades a couple times. He looks at me for guidance and I shrug. I give him a look that says, *What the fuck am I supposed to do about it?* Vargas puts the first set of clippers back in the box and plugs in the second set. He cuts Blount's hair for another minute or two before the other set of clippers overheats. Then he unplugs the second pair and goes back into the box to exchange it with the first, which hasn't had enough time to fully cool off. And so on and so forth. We're supposed to be an expeditionary force in readiness, but we're not always efficient. The clippers heat up over and over again as Vargas finishes with Blount. Then he moves on to a reluctant Johnson as I dread my turn.

"Fuck this," says Johnson throughout his haircut.

"Haunted house and a fresh haircut, all in one day," Blount says. "Lucky us." He takes Johnson's spot in the shade, rubbing his head. I just want to forget about it and pretend nothing happened. None of that shit should affect what we're here to do. What will talking about any of it change?

"It doesn't have anything to do with running an LZ, so it doesn't matter," I say.

"What about Johnson's camera? None of the pictures were there after we left."

"Just drop it," I say, annoyed that Blount knows about the camera.

"Camera's broken," says Johnson. "That's all, just a broken camera." He and I are finally on the same page, and

I need at least one person on my side if I'm going to calm everyone down.

"How do you know?" Blount asks. He scoffs. "Do you repair cameras? Did you try to take any more pictures?"

"Oh my God," Johnson says, not telling Blount about the picture he took in the backyard that turned out fine. A wise move. Mentioning that would just excite everyone even more. Then we'll never be able to get past this shit and focus.

"What about how long we were there for?" says Blount. "Did it feel like forty-five minutes to you? Come on. It felt like five minutes. That's messed up, right?"

"Five minutes? We lost track of time, man. It happens. It doesn't mean anything. You were probably just scared and your mind went weird on you."

"I wasn't fuckin' scared. How do you explain the MRE?"

"What do I have to explain?" says Johnson. "Your problem is you want to make something out of nothing because your life is boring and you got nothing to look forward to." His face is downturned so Vargas can trim the hair on the back of his neck and he glares up at Blount the same way Staff Sergeant Rynker had glared at me earlier.

"Hey, come on," I say, cutting off Blount from whatever he's about to say. He turns to me instead.

"What do you think, Corporal?"

"It was an experience," I say, which is not untrue. "That's it. Let it go before someone hears us running our mouths about it."

Then I take Johnson's place and I let Vargas singe my scalp with the molten clippers. I think about the MRE in the house and cannot come up with any explanation for what happened other than the vacuum seal must have been fucked up and something spoiled, or something alive had crawled inside by accident and died, but that all sounds like bullshit. I wouldn't believe any of that if it was someone else's explanation. If an animal got into the MRE, we would have known. We would have smelled something way sooner.

When it's Vargas's turn, I cut his hair. He doesn't get a good haircut from me, but I joke that he owes me five bucks for this one, then I laugh when he says he's charging *me* for his haircut. I wish I would've gotten to know him more during workups. He's someone I would trust to watch my back in a firefight.

I let the others walk back to our house when we're all done, then I take the shoebox back into the COC, avoiding Staff Sergeant Rynker, and I walk up the hill by the officers' house to have a look around. The dog had been up there watching us PT the other day, or at least *a* dog had been up there. But there's no dog now and I don't find any porcupine quills. I head back to our house before anyone sees me and has the chance to ask me what I'm doing.

Johnson and Blount are in the backyard, trying to fix the camera, trying to figure out what happened to all the pictures, doing anything to save themselves from the boredom that rushes back so quickly here after something unusual happens. They don't make any progress from what I can tell, but there's nothing else to do, so they keep at it for a while. Vargas tries to take a shower, but the makeshift shower in our backyard collapses and we have no way to rinse off the trimmings of hair that have worked their way under our shirts. I downplay my frustration at this to keep the others from getting riled up. Blount will never let anything go if I don't stay calm and set the example, but the itch from the haircut drives me crazy, way worse than my athlete's foot.

I wipe as much hair off with a towel as I can, but my back itches bad throughout the night, keeping me awake. The hair poking against my body starts to burn after a while, all over my skin, like a hundred porcupine quills digging in.

XVIII

The Brits launch mortar rounds from their emplacements near the front gate, a startling sound to wake to in the morning. The whole thing seems to last longer than it probably does, but it feels like forever. There's no way to sleep through it, worse than a broken fire alarm going off at the barracks. We know it's safe to get up because we aren't the ones getting shot at, but we wait in our cots anyway. We feel the drumbeats through the floor as each round goes off. If a small mortar round can shake the earth like this, the full-size howitzers are going to bring this place to the ground. The firing eventually stops and we get dressed and walk to the chow hall. We don't overhear any details about the firing mission at breakfast and no one in our group brings it up to anyone. What's there to say about it? It's just another one of those things that happens in a day here.

We finish eating, then we gear up and everyone loads in the trucks to go up to the LZ. The first group of Royal Marines is scheduled to fly out today with the lieutenant. She's heading back to Delaram and then we'll be on our own for the rest of our stint here. Arnold and Red stay behind at the FOB and let us take care of the flight on our own. They're getting too short on their tour to waste time at the LZ. We leave Vargas behind with the radio and the logbook.

We ride along the cliff roads in the trucks and park along the perimeter of the LZ. The Royal Marines pile out of their vehicles and we ask them to line up near the old excavator as if they themselves are merely cargo. They wait in a single file line, dropping their packs to the ground and sitting on top of them like chairs. The quiet morning minutes crawl by before the CH-53s reach the area and rumble towards us. We know the sound before we see them. The first bird swings around the mountain and kicks up a cloud of dust as it lands, a bloated gray whale of a helicopter with U.S. MARINES stamped on the side in dark lettering. I look up, expecting the second bird, but there's nothing. Helicopter flights always travel in pairs, so I wait for the other bird, but no. Nothing.

The lieutenant pulls her goggles down from her helmet and over her eyes. She runs across the LZ to talk to the crew chief, then she waves Blount, Johnson, and me over to her. When we get close, she points for us to climb aboard, so we run up the ramp and get on the helicopter without a question because that's what you do, especially when an officer tells you. Then we're suddenly strapped in and taking off, and all I can hear is the lieutenant yelling something about *the Taliban circling around*, which could mean anything. What are the four of us supposed to do about the Taliban? We're trained to load and unload cargo and to keep logs and to stand underneath helicopters and attach things to them.

The bird's rotor spins above us in the cargo bay. A fixture on the ceiling drips oil and grease on us. I'm strapped in too tight to avoid the drips, which leave a dark stain on my knee. We watch through the half-open cargo ramp as our helicopter's shadow dances across the desert floor below us. The black silhouette of the rear gunner contrasts with the sunlight beyond. I look from his fifty-cal down to my rifle, which I never thought I would use. We're not allowed to load them on base, and I haven't fired my M16 in-country other than to zero the sights. I haven't cleaned it in weeks, maybe more than a month. I haven't qualified on the rifle range in over a year.

"*Go condition one,*" the lieutenant shouts over the engines as loud as she can. She wants us to load a magazine and put a round in the chamber. My hands are shaking, but the lieutenant's are not. She's gung ho about this because every officer in the Marines trains to lead a small unit in combat. She's been waiting for this moment since the beginning.

I start thinking in two-word phrases. *Oh fuck. Oh Jesus.* I rip open a Velcro pouch on my flak vest and slide out a loaded magazine and then I slam it into the magazine well of my M16 and tug it to make sure it's seated properly and locked in place. I rack the charging handle to send a 5.56 round into the chamber and a cloud of dust puffs from the ejection port, so I unload the round in order to rack the handle a few more times, and more dust finds its way out. The lieutenant pretends not to notice how dirty my rifle is. Will this piece of shit even fire out here? I start thinking this could be it. Really. I want to laugh at how silly it is that we were ever distracted by a haunted house. We've always thought the worst thing here is the boredom.

I squeeze the rifle tight to stop my hands from shaking. I don't know what's about to happen, but I figure we wouldn't have gotten on the bird if we weren't meant to get back off. The bird slows and we descend as if the pilots have been reading my mind. I switch the fire selector switch on my M16 from *safe* to *fire*. Oh God. The lieutenant isn't the only one who's been waiting for this: Blount reaches out to fist-bump Johnson. He smiles and flicks his tongue out like a lizard. Johnson does not smile back. He hesitates before returning the fist bump.

"*Johnson, with me,*" shouts the lieutenant. He nods. His jaw muscles tense at the edge of his face. "*Blount, with Loyette!*" The lieutenant points to either side of the bird as she splits us into two pairs, showing which direction we'll break once we run down the ramp. We're really doing it. I think the worst thing might not be getting shot, even though that would leave my parents without both their sons, and my sister Claire without either of her brothers, and the last thing I would see before I die would be this blurry brown backdrop filled with nothing but dust and rocks. I wonder if it might be worse to be the one shooting another person. Then I would leave my family with someone totally differ-ent than whoever I'd been before, perhaps someone they wouldn't recognize. How much would that change me? But I'm ready to do it.

The helicopter drops like an elevator and my mind drifts away. I'm in preschool riding blue tricycles up and down the sidewalk with Bryce and Claire. I mold a blue and green tyrannosaurus rex out of clay. I take trips to the dunes in Michigan and make sandcastles on the beach, visit a farm and feed a brown and white horse out of my hand, go fishing in a pond and watch my uncle Hank rip their guts out on a table covered in flies. I'm bouncing a basketball against a wooden gym floor, catching a baseball in a glove, throw-ing it back to my friend Tyler. Smudged pencil sketches of

Ninja Turtles on notebook paper. Lego pieces dropping down a heat register. Math tests, spelling tests, science tests. Detention for writing swear words in school library books. A hot shower at home. A long hot shower. Losing almost every track race in high school because of shin splints, or because I was just slow. Kissing Natalie at the barn dance freshman year of college, then going a little farther than kissing Natalie after the barn dance. Wondering what she's doing now, probably studying for the LSAT or maybe even skipping class or sleeping in late on a Saturday with someone else who went farther than kissing her the night before. I see my mother's face as I leave for boot camp. My father's head-on stare as he tells me that someday I will finally need to finish something I start if I ever want to grow up and be a man. My sister's innocent smile. My brother's waxen face disappearing in the shadow of a closing casket lid. His Eagle, Globe, and Anchor pin clutched in my fingers and then flung in a rage into the woods behind our house. Everything that has ever happened to me has been a waste. What does it matter if someone ever loved me? That won't help. I imagine someone at a desk making the decisions that put me in this exact place at this exact moment. That person has no idea who I am or where I am now.

I think, *Clear tip, blurry target. Clear tip, blurry target.* This is what they train you to think on the range when you shoot at targets shaped like people. You have to stop thinking about death and start thinking about area targets and point targets and breathing control. You have to shut off everything about yourself. The bird hits the deck and my head jolts forward. The ramp drops to the dirt and I feel an ugliness inside my body pushing me towards something inevitable. I tap my finger against the side of my rifle trigger as if to the rhythm of a marching cadence and I unclip the seatbelt.

"*Let's go*," the lieutenant shouts, waving us out of the bird. We charge into the desert. I run down the ramp and break around the right side with Blount behind me. The sight of my boot touching the ground makes me wonder if the last thing Bryce saw before blowing up was his own boot, or if he died lying on his back watching birds and clouds. The sky is clear today as I run through a dust cloud flung up by the main rotor, trying not to step on a rock the wrong way and roll my ankle. Trying not to step on an old land mine. I press the buttstock of the rifle tight into my shoulder, looking just above the ACOG scope. I let the rifle barrel lead me. I can barely see through my goggles on a good day, not to mention when the air is full of dust as it now is. We can't see anything yet. If I die right now, I won't even know where I've been shot from. I wonder when the shooting will start and I think, *Clear tip, blurry target.* I imagine the dust clearing to reveal a crowd of armed men waiting for us. Then, as we run, the dust clears.

We find the other fifty-three facing us from a couple hundred feet away. Just sitting there among the rocks. It hasn't been shot down; it looks like someone landed it. There's no smoke. There's no fire. The thing is sitting there in one piece, and then I realize what this is. The bird is broken, which fucking figures. These old pieces of shit break down at Lejeune all the time. And now I'm going to die because no one could be bothered to send helicopters to Afghanistan that were not broken, because no one in charge is ever prepared for anything as obvious as this. Fuck.

"What the fuck?" Blount says as we move across the desert.

"Shut the fuck up," I say. My eyes snap back and forth. The first fifty-three takes off and leaves us behind in the desert.

"Four-corner perimeter," the lieutenant shouts from my right. She points to one side of the downed bird. "Loyette and Blount, that side! Set up at forty-five-degree angles from the front and rear of the bird." So we run to the side of the bird and I find a spot for Blount and tell him to lie down and I run to the rear corner of our square perimeter and I lie down about a hundred feet away in a position that hopefully does not put me directly in the field of fire of the fifty-cals on the bird. I push a button to let the bipod legs pop out of the broom-handle attachment on my rifle and I look down through ACOG scope. I don't know how far we've flown from the LZ, but there's nothing in sight that resembles civilization. Ahead of us lies the massive lake created by damming up the Helmand River. A mirage ripples off the water and smudges the distant horizon, causing the lake to appear as a shimmering, endless ocean. They could be here at any moment, I think. Maybe they already are.

I squirm around on the ground to find a spot where a rock isn't pushing up against my groin protector and I scan the field of fire in front of me. I can't tell if I'm seeing people moving in the distance or floaters swimming across my eyes, or maybe every blemish on the sand is just the shadow of a rock. The ACOG isn't a full-on telescope, so it's hard to tell. There's a lot of desert in front of me. The sun crawls higher into the sky as we wait in the prone position. Sweat beads up on my back and rolls down my waist. Sweat pools on my scalp and when I tip my Kevlar it runs out over my forehead in rivulets that I have to wipe off on the dirty sleeve of my cammies, which in turn smears more dirt on my face. Each slight movement of my body causes the bristles from yesterday's haircut to itch and burn against my back and I vow to shower immediately after each haircut for the rest of my life if I survive this morning. Behind me, the pilots sit in their cockpit. The gunners sit at their guns. We still don't know what the fuck's going on and the lieutenant is on the other side of the bird with Johnson. I'm coming down from the adrenaline rush and I'm thinking about all this bullshit. I could still be in college somewhere else, somewhere better than this. How fucking naive was I to think wearing a uniform would be better than school? How stupid was I to think it was worth signing up to die instead of fixing the things about my life that were broken? How stupid were any of us to think this was just an adventure? We've treated this like it's all been about sightseeing, writing blogs, posting pictures on Facebook, getting medals, tax-free pay, showing off, and telling war stories to people back home who don't know any better.

I don't know how long we're there before the pounding rotors of a Cobra helicopter echo above us. It isn't until then that I feel even a little bit safe. I keep looking through the ACOG, but if anyone tries anything they would get vaporized by the Cobra before any of us would have a chance to shoot them, and for that I feel thankful. I take a deep breath. The first fifty-three returns after making a round trip back to the LZ that takes hours. Royal Marines empty out of the bird and they gather in the spaces between the four of us. They set up machine guns and sniper rifles with barrels that seem longer than Blount's lanky body. Now the defense perimeter surrounding the bird is completely encircled, but I still feel alone. No one's closer to me than probably ten feet away, and if they were it's not like we'd be passing the time over deep conversation.

The second bird cuts its engine and the helicopter crews tinker with whatever's broken. Who knows how long they work; I don't have my watch. I thought we'd be at the LZ for a half hour tops so I didn't even bring my CamelBak. Then the second bird flies away and leaves everyone behind again, for what feels like forever until I'm startled by the lieutenant's voice behind me.

"How you doing over here, Loyette?" she asks, walking up and then lying down in the prone position next to me, continuing the exchange without looking at me. I tell her I'm fine and she hands me a plastic water bottle. "The crew had some extra water," she says. She tells me the second bird has to fly back to Leatherneck to get whatever part they need to repair the broken bird. So that's it. Their flight has to be at least an hour and a half in one direction.

"It is what it is," the lieutenant says. She walks back to her spot in the perimeter. We lie there for as long as they need us to, for as long as it takes them to fly back and forth. We wait for someone to attack the bird with AK-47s or RPGs, but no one comes because we would kill them. The Taliban are smart enough to know that, so nothing happens. I wait on the ground like a reptile basking in the sun and I try not to daydream. The repairs take at least another hour when the second bird returns, but we finally get to leave. We ride back in the broken fifty-three, kind of a sick joke. I imagine the rotor going dead during our flight, sending us straight to the ground.

When everything is sorted out and we're all dropped off, the Royal Marines and the lieutenant fly out as scheduled, and there's not much opportunity for a real goodbye, both because the departure is rushed and because that's how our relationship with her is. How would I even say goodbye to her: *Goodbye, ma'am?* That sounds stupid. Either way, she might be gone now, but she's not really absent. She was always doing her own thing.

When we get back Vargas doesn't know anything about what happened, so Blount tells him about the whole ordeal. He expresses some regret that we didn't have the opportunity to earn a combat action ribbon, which seems important to a lot of people on this deployment. You're not for real unless you have a CAR pinned to your chest. But honestly, none of that shit means anything to anyone unless you reenlist.

My back itches and I don't feel like thinking about helicopters or ribbons or the fear of death reminding me that we're part of a real live war. Johnson stumbles across the front room slowly. He hasn't said anything since we left the site of the broken-down fifty-three, nothing at the LZ or during the ride back to the FOB. I want to make sure he's okay, but I don't want to seem dramatic about it, like I care too much or like I'm the one who might not be okay.

"Hey," I say, before he can disappear into his room like he usually does.

"Yeah?" he says, glancing over his shoulder without facing towards me or putting his hands behind his back like he's supposed to.

"Did you fuck with these drawings on the wall?" I ask, not knowing what else to say, or what else to connect with him on other than the militia house. The stick figure on the wall near my cot actually does look a bit different. Maybe Johnson fucked with the drawing after all. It looks like someone changed the hair, or again, maybe I just keep remembering the drawing wrong. I would take a picture as reference if I had my own camera. The messy hair sticks out in a weird pattern, sort of poofy at the top, pointing out to the sides like fins or wings, and then oddly jutting out diagonally from the base of the head. It looks like these stupid drawings Bryce used to do as a kid. I was always better at English class, but he was the artist. It seems like everything reminds me of him these days. I wish my brother would have died in a way that wasn't constantly distracting.

"Why would I do that?" Johnson asks.

"No reason," I say, and Johnson shakes his head and walks away.

I pull off my flak vest and take off my shirt. My shoulders have already started breaking out from the sweat. I feel more disgusting than usual, which is saying a lot. Vargas and I do our best to fix the shower stall in the backyard. It kind of works. After I rinse off, I take a walk around the FOB and I find some mosquito nets left behind by the Brits. The nets are just big enough to rest on top of a cot, so I carry one back to our house and stuff my sleeping bag inside, then I drag my cot out into the backyard to sleep outside with a breeze. It feels better at first but doesn't help me to stop thinking about the things that keep me awake every night.

XIX

The nighttime breeze barely reaches me through the mosquito net. I wake up in the dark and I walk across the yard and choose a spot to piss against the back wall. We don't have anything important scheduled and the lieutenant is gone. There aren't many people around to tell us what to do, with most of the officers and senior enlisted still on their way. I don't have to wake anyone up for anything. We're OFP for the time being, on our own fucking program, so we can sleep in late. I decide to smoke a cigarette. Why not? Life here seems okay for once, even if it'll be short lived.

I climb back into the mosquito net and zip it closed around me. I close my eyes and when I reopen them I'm suspended in a black void. My boots hover over a dim source of light shining from somewhere far below me. I'm weightless, and I'm floating, submerged near the bottom of an ocean. The water is painfully cold, like frozen metal cutting my skin. My arms drift out to my sides as my uniform flaps against my body. Wads of garbage brush against my face.

The water is full of particles and pulpy debris. The current surges upward and carries me with it. The light source follows as I move. I look up to see a shape emerging from the darkness above me, a large thing that materializes into view. It's a massive shipwreck, deteriorating into brown dust as the water eats away at its surface. The bits of debris floating around me are the remnants of the ship, peeling off and floating away. I'm drifting towards a ragged gash in the hull of the ship. Piping and rusted tubes appear as the light moves closer, torn steel decks, railings and mechanical innards warped into obscene shapes that fade into the shadows within. I wave my arms and kick my legs, hoping to swim down away from it, deeper into the water. But the current pushes me up, and the ship is so vast that I won't be able to swim away without brushing against the flaking carapace of its hull. There's nothing I can do to keep myself from getting closer. The edges of the giant hole enclose my body. I don't want to touch anything, but I reach out to grab a decaying metal grate in order to steady myself. I look down to see the skin on my wrists peeling away, and beneath the surface of my skin are patches of rust that billow into the water in reddish clouds. I'm as cold as a rotting corpse. I open my mouth to scream and the particles in the water seep down into my throat and the light beneath me fades before I finally wake up in my cot shivering.

I climb out of the net and I light another cigarette and pace around our backyard in the cool night, then I sit against the perimeter wall near our shower until the others wake up and we go to breakfast. I don't say anything about the dream. What would I say about the dream if the right person was here for me to say something to, let alone one of the LS marines? There's nothing to fucking say. The others seem restless too, as if maybe they also lost sleep last night, but I don't ask anyone if they're okay.

XX

Arnold and Red take us to go swimming behind the dam. The rest of the Brits are leaving today, but there's enough time for our new friends to show us their secret spot near the LZ. We continue our habit of not informing Staff Sergeant Rynker when we leave the FOB. This time we leave through the front gate, right in front of his face, although he would probably assume we were going to the LZ anyway. After the long, winding ride, Arnold doesn't turn left towards the LZ at the end of the dam. Instead, he turns right and we coast down a gravel slope that leads to the lake like a boat ramp, as if people go fishing here early on Saturday mornings. The water is bright green and too cloudy to see anything beneath the surface. I try not to imagine what's down there, but it's impossible not to imagine a shipwreck after the dream last night.

We stage our gear on the ground in a neat row, then Blount and Vargas strip to their skivvy shorts and they dive in right away. They gasp when they resurface, shocked by the iciness of the water on such a hot day. Red takes off his boots and then jumps in. Johnson wades in slowly and cries out as the water reaches his chest. I pull off my boots and socks and dip my feet in, but the water is so cold it feels like teeth biting me. I pull my feet out of the water and I thumb off chunks of dead yellow skin from between my toes. Arnold sits on the rocks next to me and looks at my feet.

"Tasty," he says, which makes me laugh. It's good to laugh about things that are obviously not funny. I guess you have to learn that in the military. Arnold asks if us lads are ready to take over the LZ on our own, so I shrug.

"We're about to find out," I say.

"You'll be fine," says Arnold, which I know, but it would feel stupid to be too confident about anything at this point. Running the LZ is simple but who knows what's going to happen over the next couple weeks before we go back to Delaram. Hopefully nothing at all, but you never know. Arnold's wearing sunglasses, but I can tell he's watching the others in the water, making sure they're distracted as they goof off and splash each other before he speaks. Then he turns to me.

"What happened in the house?" Arnold asks. We haven't talked with the Brits about any of that since it happened. No one has asked.

"I don't know. We lost track of time," I say, which is true.

"Aye, happened to us," says Arnold after thinking about it. "Once is enough in there; don't go back. Just do your time and forget it." Another quiet moment passes by, then he finally says, "We lost a mate because of it."

"Lost? What do you mean?"

"Well, not dead, but I had to send him home."

"Jesus," I say. "You scared the shit out me."

"Sorry," Arnold says. "I have no memory of going inside." He turns his face towards me and then back to the water. He grins to himself. "Best to be quick if you go in, then come out right away." He drums his fingers on his knees, playing an invisible piano. "Don't know what that place is about, but I don't like it. Should've torn it down first thing."

"Did you go in the basement?" I ask, wondering how none of this ever came up in conversation before.

"Basement?" says Arnold. "Don't remember any basement." The others are doing their own thing in the water, so they don't hear as he continues. "We went in to have a look, found our way out. Most of us were fine, but we had to send one off before he caused a panic. Couldn't do his job. Couldn't sleep. Couldn't eat, he said." Arnold shakes his head.

"Then why did you let us go in?" I ask. "Weren't you afraid it would happen to us?"

"Well," says Arnold. "I thought our bloke was just trying to get sent home. I thought it was *bullshit*, as you Yanks put it."

"It probably is."

"Maybe, maybe not."

"So what are we supposed to do about it?"

"Bugger all," says Arnold, shrugging.

Blount calls out to me from the water, tells me to get in, but I say I'm good. I'm not getting in the water if I can't see what's in it. Swimming would be appealing on any day but today. I wonder about the shipwreck dream and I open my mouth to mention it to Arnold, but I don't want him worried about us on the day he leaves to go home. I don't want him to think I'm a wanker, as the Brits put it. Blount splashes water, but none of it reaches me. I don't say anything else, but this little afternoon outing feels wrong. We were just out in the desert waiting to get shot at, and now we're taking a break from the whole war to sit back and relax. We might as well enjoy it while we're here, but I don't think we'll be coming back to go swimming.

Some fish splash at the surface. Birds fly overhead. It's nice and quiet. Kajaki is a combat zone, but I wonder if it would rather not be. Sometimes a place just wants to be a place in the world. I wonder what it was like here when they first built the dam.

Blount says he keeps stubbing his toe on *something*. I wish he would just say he's stubbing his toe on rocks. He and Vargas drift a bit too far away the next few minutes as they get caught up in splashing each other. I tell them to come back and get dressed.

"Your farmer's tan is offensive," I yell at Blount. "Cover it up before you blind me."

We ride back to the FOB so Arnold and Red can pack up the rest of their personal gear and prepare to leave. Most of the Brit gear is packed up now. We can't watch the World Cup anymore since they took the TV out of the chow hall and sealed it in a box. Before they go, I trade an extra Gerber to Red for a pair of his camouflage shorts, even though I won't be able to wear them until I'm back in the States. Maybe someone will see me wearing them years from now and recognize where I got them from and I'll get a free beer out of it. Who knows? Blount and Vargas trade Red for some British unit patches that we'll probably keep tucked away in boxes for the rest of our lives, waiting for a random moment to share these artifacts with friends or family. We exchange emails and Facebook pages and promise to play *Call of Duty* online with them after we all get home. Then I offer to take a picture of everyone standing together with Johnson's camera. The picture turns out fine. I think about asking Red to corroborate what Arnold said about the militia house, but I figure he'll just tell me the same things he's already told me.

The Brits load up in a couple green CH-47s at the LZ. The flight is scheduled to take a net load, so one of the birds hovers across to us after taking off with passengers and we hook up the cargo in the downwash, as we've been doing. I make eye contact with Red through the hellhole on the bottom of the bird. He's strapped in a seat next to Arnold, finally getting out of here. We wave goodbye and they wave back at us through the opening as the forty-seven raises up and up, then it disappears and we can hear the sound until it fades away into the desert as if someone is turning a volume dial to zero. And that's it. Now we're all out of friends. We're alone with the porcupine quills and the militia house, and soon the artillery battery and more officers and staff NCOs and all the bullshit that comes with them, which is worse than any haunted house could ever be. The only thing we have to look forward to now is the day we finally get to leave.

XXI

The FOB is exceptionally lonely for a day or two. Right now it's occupied only by the advance party marines and our small squad. Still, none of us are looking forward to the arrival of the rest of the artillery battery. We like it this way, so we celebrate our last night of freedom by using what's left of Johnson's laptop battery to watch *Don't Be a Menace* with the volume turned up as loud as it goes. It's so loud a couple advance party marines hear us from the next house. They stop by and lean in our door to watch some of the movie. We invite them inside, but they thank us for the offer and head back to their house. It feels good to forget about everything happening outside the glowing borders of the computer screen, as if nothing else matters until the movie ends, but I find myself stealing glances at the graffiti in the corner, the ship and the stick figure. Neither has moved since I last checked, so I try to focus on the movie instead of being paranoid. It feels good to laugh at slapstick humor, even if we don't laugh as much as we would if we were watching the movie under other circumstances. We don't get interrupted by any radio calls from the COC, a small miracle.

It's late when we finish the movie. I go out back to brush my teeth. The sky is clear and the moon shines even brighter than Johnson's computer screen. I spit out a wad of toothpaste and watch it land on the ground next to a banded porcupine quill. I look to make sure, but I don't find any others. Vargas is asleep when I go back inside. I wake him up and I make him show me the porcupine quill he took from the militia house. He's groggy but he does what I ask. He opens the zipper on his daypack and shows me his porcupine quill and then asks if he can go back to sleep and I tell him yes. He probably won't remember this in the morning. At least I hope not. I take the souvenir from his daypack and the needle from the backyard and I toss them both over the back wall. They land somewhere on the other side, out of sight, out of mind.

II

XXII

Another day goes by. Then we're at the LZ again. This time we're waiting for the artillery unit to show up. We wait until two fifty-threes fly in thirty minutes late, each of them hauling a tan, up-armored Humvee dangling from a cargo sling. The birds take turns hovering in low to drop off each vehicle on the gravel, their engines powered up, blasting debris. They blow shit everywhere across the LZ and against the guard-house overlooking the plateau. Some random belongings shoot away from the guardhouse, carried away by the rotor downwash. The first and second Humvees drop down and bounce against the gravel when the birds cut the hook. The guards shout at us from the hill after the first flight leaves, but they retreat inside as the second flight closes in. The next pair of birds hovers low over the house again, as if the pilots can't simply open their eyes. They land and drop their ramps and out pours the first wave of the artillery battery in their clean desert MARPAT utility uniforms. They gather in formation near the old crane. Now we outnumber the local guards by a couple hundred; they won't be coming down here to complain about what our helicopters are doing to their house.

It takes a couple more trips for the fifty-threes to drop off the marines throughout the morning, and since they only dropped two Humvees, it'll take all day to drive back and forth and bring the passengers down to the FOB. You'd think everyone could just hump it along the road, but that would make too much sense. So I guess we'll be up here for a few hours waiting our turn to go back.

The new arrivals keep their helmets on, but I imagine all of them having high and tights hidden underneath. They all look excited, some of them smiling as if they're about to have a great old time here. Fucking new guys, their wide-eyed enthusiasm gives them all away.

"Let's go," shouts a corporal to some junior marines filing out of the helicopters. They gather in formation together in an orderly fashion. "Hurry up!"

"Ruh-ruh-roger that," some of them shout in response. Blount looks at me like they're speaking another language.

"Huh?" he says to me.

"No idea," I say. "I only work here." If I told someone *ruh-ruh-roger that*, then I would get taken aside and corrected, but I don't know. I guess they think they're cool and laid-back like that.

The officers and staff NCOs stand away from the bulk of their enlisted marines. They glance sideways at me and my marines like they own the place, like we don't belong, like we're the intruders. Shit, they don't even know. We haven't washed our uniforms since before we got here. They're probably scrutinizing us for that, but they'll know what it's like soon. They'll fit in once they've had enough time to get sick of this place.

These are our first inbound passengers, I realize, the first since we've started running the LZ. I have to make sure

Vargas takes the ID of each artillery marine and writes their names down in our green logbook as they wait for a ride to the FOB. That way I can transfer everything from the logbook to the SIPRNet later. Supervising, once again, my new lot in life.

When most of the artillery marines have been driven down to the FOB, we finally get our turn in the back of a Humvee and we ride down to the FOB, packed in with a bunch of annoying new guys who are still left over. As we ride back along the road, I realize we've made history, like the lieutenant first told me. We're the first landing support marines to come here and run the LZ. No one else in our platoon can say shit to us; they haven't been here. They haven't been the first to do anything. But somehow, I don't feel any different about anything than I normally do. I don't feel suddenly proud.

Later, we get a call on our radio from Staff Sergeant Rynker. He says I need to be at the COC this evening for a special briefing. Attendance is required for all section heads, and I guess I'm a section head now that the lieutenant's gone. I take my blue notebook with me, and I head over to the briefing room to hear whatever needs to be said in front of a room full of section heads, lieutenants, and senior enlisted. I haven't been in a meeting like this before. I don't know what could be said in a meeting that would change any of the fundamentals of my job. As it turns out, none of the other section heads are below the rank of sergeant. When I walk into the briefing room, they glare at me as if I don't belong. There are several benches, but no one gets up to make any room for me to sit down. I'm the one who would have to make room for them.

"Good evening, gentlemen," I say. They watch as I make

my way to the back of the room, and then I get a pen out
to take notes. Everyone stands up for the captain when he
walks in, as if he were a judge walking into the courtroom.
You think a captain is going to be like the officers in war
movies who turn out to be teachers or lawyers halfway
through, but they're not as smart as they seem. In real life
they either have no personality or they're just football jocks
you have to salute. I've never met the Tom Hanks version of
a captain.

"Take a seat, gents. At ease," says the captain, waving his
hand for everyone to sit back down. "Welcome to Kajaki,
erruh?"

"*Erruh!*" replies the room full of new people. The *ooh-rah*
feels foreign to me after spending so much time around the
Brits, never hearing anyone shout it like you do all the time
on an American base. This is a room full of people excited to
finally be in a war. Maybe some of the older ones are returning for a second or third time. They're ready to blow people
up and earn some medals.

"I'm Captain Connors, for those of you who don't know
me, which I'm pretty sure you all do," says the captain, even
though I don't. He has a big, square head with a jaw like a
snowplow. The wall behind him is one big map of the AO,
dots representing all of the villages and bases in the Helmand
Province. He paces back and forth like a general pumping up
an invasion force.

"I'm a hard charger, gents," he says. "I'm here to make
sure we do this job right, do justice to Operation Herrick as
we build up this FOB. We've got a lot to do, gents. Nothing
new. But that's how we like it, check? It is what it is. We
should have all the sections represented here, the guns, bulk
fuelers, food service . . ." He trails off.

"Landing support, sir," says Staff Sergeant Rynker, slouching on one of the benches. He reaches his arm back and points directly at me, turning his head to stare. The others turn in their seats to have a better look, all eyes in the room targeting me. The sergeants and staff sergeants stare at me for no reason, ignoring the captain. A minute goes by. Staff Sergeant Rynker doesn't introduce me. No one addresses me.

"That's the one?" Captain Connors finally says. The others keep their eyes on me.

"Yes, sir," says Staff Sergeant Rynker.

What the fuck is he talking about? *That's the one?* What's that supposed to mean? Captain Connors stares at me another moment and then clears his throat loudly. The section heads turn to face him, back to ignoring me again. The captain holds out his arms and yells, "Anyway, who's ready to blow shit up, *erruh?*"

"*Erruh, sir!*"

The captain moves on and everyone acts like nothing weird happened. They ignore me for the rest of it. The captain paces back and forth in front of the room, giving a TED Talk on blowing people up in the desert while I wonder what the fuck Staff Sergeant Rynker has already told him about me. What would there be to say? Unless he knows we went to the militia house, but if he knows we went, why hasn't he burned us for it yet? The captain tells us more of what we already know about the mission here. He keeps calling us *gents.*

"I will pursue this mission aggressively, with or without you, gents, but I want you with me, gents," he says. "I need you with me, Marines. Marines, our first order of business is to clear out all the brush from the yards at the houses on the west end of the FOB. This is our number one priority. We can't have anything flammable near the guns and ammunition, *erruh*?"

"*Erruh, sir*," shout the section heads. I have my notebook open to take notes but I've written nothing. If there was nothing to write before, the CO has given me nothing to write now. Nothing he says applies to landing support, except ripping out the grass at the row of houses where we live. We have to help clear the grass, which means they're going to be putting the guns near our house. I guess we can use the forklift to pull out all the dirt and dead grass. We'll have to move our gear somewhere else, sleep somewhere else. We'll probably move to the barracks by the east side of the FOB near the front gate where the artillery battery lives. Everyone will love the news.

"Man, fuck that," says Johnson when I tell him I want him to till up the yard tomorrow so we can get rid of the dead grass.

"We can't say no to them," I say. "You either use the forklift or you help us pull the grass out by hand."

"This is stupid," Blount says.

"You should be used to that by now," I say, and then, "Vargas isn't complaining. Why don't you be more like him." Vargas leans forward on the edge of his cot with his hands folded, elbows resting on his knees. He shrugs without adding anything. We leave it at that and get ready to go to sleep.

I climb inside the mosquito net on my cot and I zip it shut. Everything about my life revolves around waking up and going to sleep. We live from day to day, meal to meal. The night is the only time we have left to spend alone with ourselves. I lie on my back for a while, until I hear Vargas whispering again. Then I fall asleep and dream I'm running through the militia house, firing an AK-47 into a group of advancing men who charge at us through the smoke. Men drop to the floor in bloody piles. The gunfire fucks up my hearing until all that's left is a ringing intonation building in my head.

Spent shell casings tumble through the air and rain against my face. One slips under my shirt collar and lodges against my shoulder and sears the skin around my collar bone. When I reach in to sweep the hot brass out of my shirt, I notice I'm wearing a Soviet uniform. The smoke fills the stairwell, creeps into my nostrils, spills down my throat. We're all cornered in a room together. There's nowhere left to go. Through the smoke I watch my comrade pull a side-arm from a side holster and blow his brains out, the inside of his head splashing against the wall in an instant. The smoke seeping into me is not smoke; it's a swarm of flies pushing into my mouth. The ringing in my ears is not a simple tone but a voice shrieking, the sound escalating until the men chasing us reach the doorway with their knives drawn.

I shudder awake in my cot and my mouth tastes like ash. I can't hear my own cough because my ears are still ringing. But how can that be? Why are my ears still ringing? My collar bone burns too. When I reach up and tap the spot where the hot brass burned me in the dream, my skin there feels tender and sore, prickly. The aching, itching skin between my toes pulses as if something is trying to punch its way through from inside. It was just a dream, that's it. I get up and chug water from my CamelBak to wash the taste out of my mouth, but that doesn't work so I brush my teeth again.

The clouds block the moon and it's too dark to see anything in the backyard, but I notice a figure in the dark standing there, a person near the perimeter wall in the backyard of the neighboring house. Someone waiting. It's a marine wearing a skivvy shirt and camouflage trousers. It's not that he's out of place; the FOB is full of marines. But there's something eerie about him. I can't see which way he's facing. I keep still, hold the toothbrush still. It's the middle of the night and as quiet as it's ever been, but I hear the ground crunch as the figure's weight shifts from one boot to the other. He doesn't take a step. I spit out a mouthful of toothpaste and wipe my mouth.

"Hello?" I say. He doesn't answer. He takes a step towards me, and then another. I'm not sure what to do, but then I see that it's Vargas, and I say, "Hey." He stops moving.

"Oh, good evening, Corporal," he says. "I didn't see you."

"What were you doing over there?" I say. "You looked like you were walking to the back gate."

"Um," says Vargas. Then, as if remembering something specific, he reaches down and buttons up his pants. "I was making a head call." I notice his boots are tied. If you were going to walk outside really quick and then come right back, you wouldn't need to tie your boots all the way.

"Well, don't piss in their backyard," I say. "I'll have to hear about it at one of the section head meetings if they find out." The night is silent before Vargas answers.

"Good to go, Corporal," he says, but I press the issue before he can walk away.

"You know you talk in your sleep," I say. "Did you know that?"

"What?"

"Yeah, I hear you whispering like a weirdo."

"Oh," says Vargas. "No, not talking in my sleep. I'm just praying before bed. I've always done that."

"I thought you didn't believe in God," I say. Vargas doesn't answer and I eventually grunt to let him know he can leave. He walks back inside. I climb back in my cot again and I listen for a while, but this time I don't hear any whispering.

XXIII

I watch Vargas the next few days, but he doesn't give me any reason to worry. Some of the artillery marines come by to help us clear the vegetation from around our house, and Vargas helps out along with everyone else, nothing out of the ordinary. He never complains about busy work anyway. He and Blount end up making friends with some of the artillery juniors and they sit together at noon chow and gossip like it's lunchtime back in grade school. I watch them from across the chow hall. Blount still nervously opens his MREs as if something's about to reach out from inside and grab him.

I eat with one of the artillery NCOs, this dude I met named Corporal Garza. He's one of the FNGs who just flew in, but he's okay, even though all he talks about is how bad he wants some gun time. That's how they all are, and I don't have anything to contribute to that conversation. I just want the big guns to fly in so we can leave. We eat our food and I ask him why his junior marines respond to him with that weird phrase I keep hearing.

"What's this *ruh-ruh-roger that* shit?" I ask him. "Everyone says it like it's normal. Is that like a unit thing or something?" Garza shakes out a little bottle of Tabasco sauce into the pouch holding his spaghetti main course and then he stirs it up with a brown plastic spoon. He grins and starts nodding his head to an imaginary beat.

"Nicki Minaj," he says. "She's blowing up back home, dude. She's in pretty much every song." He laughs. "And she has a fat ass, yo. I don't know what she's more famous for, that or the music."

"Oh," I say. "Weird." I wonder what else has happened in the States since we've been gone. How many new celebrities are there? We're making history over here, but all the history back home is passing us by. I guess we have a lot of catching up to do when we get back. About seven months' worth of catching up. I guess my list starts with Nicki Minaj.

After lunch, we get word on the radio that Staff Sergeant Rynker wants to see me at the COC, probably something about a flight coming up, hopefully the flight carrying in the howitzers. But when I walk into the COC I find him waiting for me alone in the briefing room where the section head meetings are, sitting on one of the benches and leaning against the wall. He's got my blue notebook open on his lap, the notebook I've been using for the meetings, the notebook that's always in my daypack. How the fuck did he get a hold of it? He smiles at me and waves me closer and looks at me awhile before speaking.

"Corporal Loyette," he finally says. "How's the journalism business treating you?"

"I don't know, Staff Sergeant," I say. What does he mean by that? Did he find a way to access the old blog? I took all of that offline so no one would be able to find it again no matter how hard they searched; that was one of the agreements I made with the lieutenant to get off with only a page eleven in my SRB. I'm liable to get in trouble again if it's still available.

"You don't know," says Staff Sergeant Rynker. "But it seems to me that you *do* know." He looks down into the pages of the notebook, which are filled with handwritten text. I don't remember writing that much since we've arrived, so that's weird. And all the other material from when I wrote the blog had been torn out and thrown away. I only remember jotting down notes and other reminders to myself about flights at the LZ. Staff Sergeant Rynker begins reading from the pages while I stand in front of him horrified:

"*Dear General McChrystal*"—he starts off by reading each word carefully, glances up at me, then back down at the notebook—"*Are high-and-tights popular in the army? Probably not. Soldier hair always looks normal to me whereas we look like a bunch of dumbasses when we're within regulation standards. Do they handle it differently for soldiers in the army? Or do generals just get to do whatever they want whenever they want? That's what it seems like. I can't even imagine, sir. That must be nice. Good for you. You should come help us on the flight line sometime. I know officers like to get their hands dirty to fit in with the enlisted, right? They like to get down in the shit to look tough. Make sure to bring your EarPro; it gets loud at the LZ, like spending a few hours in a nightclub. Come on down. We'll show you around, show you a good time. There's a lot of stuff to do here. Sincerely and with so much respect I can't even contain it all, Corporal Loyette.*"

My heart is racing when he finally stops because he's reading a passage that had originally been posted on my blog. I first wrote the entry in my notebook like most of the others and then transcribed it to the internet, but I threw those pages out just like the others. I even did that back in Delaram.

"I don't know what that has to do with journalism," I say.

"Don't be a fuckin' smart-ass," says Staff Sergeant Rynker. He closes the notebook and leans his head back against the wall and says, "Okay, I'll admit some of that trash about officers is true. They do dumb shit to make friends with their NCOs like spear feral cats or whatever crazy shit I saw in Iraq. So great job, but are you really planning to show people this shit?"

"No, Staff Sergeant," I say, thankful for the simple yes or no question. I was trying to think of a story to make up if he asked me to explain myself, but he's saving me the trouble. The problem is it seems like he might already know about my blog, but it's hard for me to tell. If he does, I can't believe the lieutenant would have mentioned anything about that to him. What purpose would it serve? I feel betrayed thinking she might have left me here saddled with baggage from back when I was a junior marine. I still don't even know how he got the notebook. Did I leave it here by accident? I always make sure it's in my daypack.

"How old do you think I am?" asks Staff Sergeant Rynker. I don't answer right away and he says, "Pick a number."

"Thirty-four, Staff Sergeant," I say, providing the first honest answer that comes to mind. I could go older, but thirty-four works.

"Thirty-four?" he says. "Well fuck you too. You know, your lieutenant told me to keep an eye on you when you're on the fuckin' computer."

"Aye aye, Staff Sergeant," I say. It's all I can think to say. Staff Sergeant Rynker stares at me and then flings the notebook like a Frisbee and I catch it using both hands. He laughs at how stupid I look trying not to drop the notebook.

"Y'all eat our food and sleep in our beds and you act like we're your damn maids. Don't leave your trash lying around the COC again and don't write bullshit on the internet," he says, as if we're intruding in a place we're not welcome. I never begged anyone to come here, I think, as he keeps going. "LS squad," he says. "Has kind of a ring to it, huh? *LS Squad. Kickin' ass and takin' names!*" He laughs, then waits a moment before asking, "You like to draw too, don't you, or are you just the next Stephen King?"

"Draw, Staff Sergeant?" I say, and then, "Not really."

"Yeah right," he says, then laughs again. "Taking me for a fuckin' moron, huh? Get the fuck outta here."

I give Staff Sergeant Rynker the proper greeting and I stalk across the FOB back to the house. The others are lounging on the cots inside, complacent motherfuckers, like it's their living room back home. They look soft and lazy when I hold my notebook out for them to see. Someone must have seen the blog months ago and saved it, then copied it from that source onto the pages to fuck with me. How else could this have happened?

"Who did this?" I say, and they stare back like I'm talking to someone who's standing behind them. "Who put this in the COC? Who wrote this shit?" I open the notebook to the page with the letter to McChrystal and I toss it at them. Vargas holds up his hands to block the notebook from hitting his face and I regret coming off so aggressive. I don't think it was him. It could be any of the three, but I don't think it was Blount either. He and Vargas are both stuck with me after we leave here, at least until they send me back to my permanent unit, so why would they burn a bridge and stir shit up? And I don't think it was Johnson either. He doesn't have to deal with me again after this. He gets to go back to his own platoon, but he doesn't strike me as the one to waste energy being an asshole.

"It's not in my handwriting," he says. He holds the notebook out for me to come get.

"Stand up when you talk to me," I say. Johnson stands up, his arm still outstretched for me to take the notebook from him. I snatch it from his hand.

I tell them, "This is not the time or place to fuck around," and I wonder who I'm really saying it to, them or myself. I head back to the other side of the FOB, next to the COC where we've got a perpetual trash fire going in a rusted barrel. I toss in the notebook and watch it catch on fire without reading the rest of the words. Fuck it. I don't need an extra notebook anyway. We've got the green logbook for everything official. I look over my shoulder, but no one's watching, then I walk back to our house where Blount meets me at the front.

"Everything's cool," I say. "I burned it."

"It wasn't any of us, Corporal," he says. He looks surprised. "Honest."

"Fine," I say. I believe him, but I don't want to show weakness by apologizing.

XXIV

The triple sevens finally show up on the flight tracker. It's good for us to have something to focus on after the shit with the notebook. We drive up to the LZ and wait for the birds. I don't say much to the junior marines while we sit around, still embarrassed about calling them out for something I don't think any of them did. Maybe it doesn't matter with the notebook burned. There's one less way for someone to fuck with me now, so I don't have to worry about it again.

While we wait, we overhear the Taliban talking on an Icom radio in the Humvee. We only know it's Taliban because the driver tells us, otherwise it just sounds like two dudes talking on a shitty radio. They don't sound like terrorists. They sound like a bunch of stoners, toking up and taking turns laughing, not angry like I thought they would sound. Blount and Vargas gather around the open Humvee door with me, and we let the words wash over us. They could be saying anything. They could be damning us all to hell. I've never seen any Taliban in person, at least not that I know. Hopefully it stays that way. Their conversation goes on for a while until the helicopters drown it out.

The fifty-threes fly in low with the guns strapped up in slings, swaying around like captive beasts. The birds' rotors are turned up to carry the heavy load and they send all kinds of debris flying at us, trashing the guardhouse once again. We run behind the old yellow crane to take shelter and a few artillery marines follow to join us. I peek around the edge of the crane to watch as the birds drop the guns down on the gravel. The guns are olive drab and each has two wheels set in their lowered configuration so they can be towed like trailers. The tires of the first gun bounce against the ground and the bird cuts the load. The sling drops from the hook and collapses on the gravel next to the gun. Then a series of white projectiles shoots silently from the side of the bird, vaguely in our direction. The white flares leave smoke trails as they sail past us and over the edge of the cliff towards the river. I spin back towards Blount and bump into him. His eyes are closed behind his goggles. He's crouched against the crane with his head down, fidgeting with a twig on the ground. He hasn't even seen the flares.

We run out and unchain the slings from each of the three guns. One of the birds lands and we drag the slings up the cargo ramp and coil them in piles in order to send them back to their origin point. Then we run back down the ramp and the birds take off. Corporal Garza walks up to the gun nearest to me. The drone of the fifty-three rotors trails off as he kneels and runs a gloved hand along the green surface of the gun. He doesn't seem to notice me until I break him out of the trance he's fallen into.

"Hey, what the hell was that crap that shot out the side of the bird?"

"No idea," Garza says after he looks up at me. His junior marines encircle the guns and maneuver them around to hitch them up to the backs of the Humvees. Garza shrugs. "Must have been radios in the trucks setting them off. Interference. Some kind of signal."

Johnson tells us he read on Wikipedia that the Marines have been using fifty-threes since Vietnam. That figures, I think. It would explain why they're always broken. We ride back down to the FOB with everyone, sitting in back of the Humvees. We watch the guns bounce around on the cliffside road as they follow behind us.

The artillery marines drive us into the FOB and pull up to our row of houses. They drop their blouses and skivvy shirts on the ground, and one at a time they unhitch the guns and roll them into the yard along the back wall. The marines adjust the wheels on the guns and then unfold the legs, which unfold like the legs of a giant mantis, two spindly legs out in front and two sturdy legs in back with spades on them like giant green paws digging into the dirt. They set up the guns facing west towards the Green Zone and leave them in a dormant state with canvas covers fastened over their muzzles. Staff Sergeant Rynker walks up to us after they're finished. He stares at me. Enough time passes by for one of the other artillery marines to approach him with a question.

"Excuse me, Staff Sergeant," says the marine. "I have a question." When Staff Sergeant Rynker doesn't respond, the marine looks from Staff Sergeant Rynker to me, and then back again before giving up and walking away shaking his head.

"This place is private property now," he finally says. "Y'all need to take your gear to the barracks by the COC where everyone else lives. Been over here gaffing off in your own house. LS squad ain't so special anymore." He narrows his eyes at me from under the shade of his eight-point cover.

"And having you right next door might be a good thing." He walks away and laughs so everyone can hear. A group of corporals and sergeants joins him and they walk down the road together like a gang of bullies, turning a corner and then heading back to the COC.

"What's he mean by that, Corporal?" asks Blount.

"I honestly don't know," I say.

We go out back and sit with the guns after the artillery marines are all gone. I think about how much I'll miss our secluded setup. We managed to have our own house for about a month. Not bad. I wish anyone cared about us as much as they cared about the triple sevens. They sit quietly, their covered barrels pointed down towards the perimeter wall. If the guns are here, that means we're done. Our mission is over. We came here to keep a logbook up to date for a few weeks and now we can go back to Delaram. The only thing they need here is their ammunition and that should be it. I don't want to be here when they shoot off the howitzers for the first time. We've heard explosions throughout the deployment, usually the EOD guys blowing up captured UXO out in the desert, but these guns look fucking loud.

"Fuck man, I don't want to move my shit again," Blount says. "Kandahar, Delaram, here. It never ends. Man, I like this house. This house is fucking fine."

"It's not that big of a deal," Johnson says. "You got what, three bags? Main pack, seabag, daypack? Come on, we're just carrying it across the FOB. It's like a quarter mile."

"Psh, whatever."

"I'll carry your seabag, fool," Vargas says.

"No, that's not what I meant," says Blount.

I ignore them and I walk back to the COC to see if the TACC has the howitzer ammunition scheduled on the flight tracker. It's the only thing left. That would give me a better idea of how much longer we have left here, how much longer we have to put up with the militia house and the porcupine quills and the flies.

I sit down at one of the open laptops and I log in to check the tracker. The ammo flights are easy to spot on the spreadsheet. The tactical air control officer makes a habit of highlighting the cells in red if the cargo includes live ammunition, anything dangerous or hazardous like that, so it's easy to spot right away. But I don't see any flights scheduled for us in the upcoming days. Three howitzers and no plans to send any rounds? Then what's the point of sending them here? It doesn't make sense but nothing surprises me. I slide over to one of the phones and I call down to our company ops office in Delaram. I'm calling during normal business hours, so the lieutenant should be around. She doesn't pull the twelve-hour shifts like everyone else. She works during the day. The phone rings a few times and then someone picks up.

"Ops office, Corporal Melton speaking. How can I help you, sir or ma'am?" says Corporal Melton, who's one of the last people in the platoon I'm in the mood to speak with. Melton's treated me like crap since I got my temporary orders to join the platoon. Why do they have an NCO answering the phone anyway? I want to lie and tell him I'm a sergeant major or a colonel, but I'd rather just get to the point and find out when we can come back.

"It's Loyette," I say. "Is the ma'am around?" A moment of hesitation on the other end before Melton speaks. I hear another voice or two in the background, other company staff speaking to each other in the office. I can't tell if either voice is the lieutenant's.

"Yes," he says.

"Can you go get her?"

Melton waits a moment and then says, "How's Kajaki, dude? How long has it taken you to fuck something up? Leave your rifle somewhere? Crash a Humvee?"

He lists off these items as if I'm known to leave my rifle in places or crash Humvees, neither of which I've ever done. I glance over my shoulder to see if anyone else is in the COC with me, Staff Sergeant Rynker or anyone else in the battery command element. There's one artillery marine entering data into a standard green logbook, but that's it.

"Motherfucker, just get the lieutenant," I say. I take a deep breath and Melton tells me he'll get the ma'am but I probably won't like what she has to say. He sings the last words to me before I hear the phone drop on the desk and I hear him telling the lieutenant I'm on the phone.

"Lieutenant Guerrero," says the lieutenant.

"Good afternoon, ma'am," I say. "It's Corporal Loyette."

"How'd everything go with the guns? I heard they finally made it."

"Great, ma'am. Great. I was just calling to let you know everything went great. Everything's good to go. Uh, I was looking to see when we should expect to fly back down to Delaram." I imagine the clean bathrooms back at Delaram, the hot showers, the food at the chow hall. No more MREs. The air-conditioned tents with real mattresses where you can get a solid night's rest. They've got these refrigerators set up around the FOB where you can walk in and grab a cold bottle of water anytime you want. Someone else can deal with this place now. The lieutenant clears her throat. I don't feel like there's anything she can say that would surprise me at this point.

"Unfortunately, it looks like we'll need you all there until pretty much the end of the deployment," she says. So that's it. That would mean another month. "I'm sorry to say the relief for our battalion isn't going to be here until the end of July as it turns out, so we need to cover the LZ in Kajaki until then."

"Good to go, ma'am," I say immediately, but I'm not really good to go. Another month here? I just breathe into the phone receiver at first. It's like being abandoned. First she leaves, then we have to stay longer. I wonder how the others will react to the news. Vargas won't say much. Blount will complain. Johnson will probably keep his thoughts to himself.

"It is what it is," the lieutenant says. "It's what we're here to do, so it's what we're going to do." There's an edge to her voice, but without interacting in person it's hard to tell exactly how to read her. If she's annoyed, then so be it. It's her job to make sure I know what's going on.

"Good to go, ma'am," I say again, and then, "We'll get it done. Our job is to make shit happen." She doesn't ask what my thoughts are or if I have any questions, and she doesn't really ask me how I feel or if we're doing all right. It doesn't matter if we're okay because how we feel would never change anything. That's nothing new. However, she does ask if we need anything, and I tell her I'm sure the junior marines would love it if she could send us some Rip Its or some Gatorade. Anything with sugar in it. She says she'll see what she can do, and I tell her good afternoon again and then we're done talking. I walk back to the house. The others react as I predicted. Blount goes out into the yard and throws rocks against the wall. Vargas joins him, but not because he's angry too. He finished his Harry Potter book and now he's bored. Johnson tries not to react, but he can't help it, sulking for the rest of the day. He's stuck with us.

"One month down," Blount says. "What's another month? Another fuckin' month! Shouldn't make any difference, right?"

"No, it shouldn't," I say, and Blount turns around, not realizing I had been watching. He drops the next rock he was about to throw.

The three of them spend the rest of the afternoon batting the big hornets out of the air again. Then they make holes in the dirt and pour in hand sanitizer before lighting the hornets on fire. Their response is far from healthy, but at least they're dealing with it together.

XXV

We're at the LZ at night. The artillery marines are on a patrol in the Green Zone. Lucky them. We listen to the distant popping of small arms fire and watch orange tracer rounds streak into the sky. The sound of the gunfire is hollow and plain. The tracer rounds we don't see must be hitting their targets, I think. My daypack is lying on the ground and I lean back against it with my flak on, which isn't a bad way to stay propped up if you want to fall asleep without lying down. There are only three of us up here tonight: Johnson, Blount, and me. Vargas is back at the FOB with our radio again. We don't need to bring everyone up here all the time, and between Blount and Vargas, I'm more worried about keeping Blount busy.

After a while, a flight of two fifty-threes drowns out the distant small arms fire as they hover in and land on the opposite side of the plateau from us. They drop off a few tri-walls, which are really just big cardboard boxes, so it's nothing complicated for us to deal with. Johnson brings the forklift in close behind the bird while the loadmaster guides him with hand signals, keeping him from running into the tail rotor as he gets close enough to extend the tines into the cargo bay. A sudden gust of wind almost blows a tri-wall right to the ground, but Blount is close enough to run and shove it back on the forks. I wait in the dark with my arms folded. Blount can take care of this shit on his own. I don't even have to supervise. Johnson gets out of the forklift to help Blount after that. He's learned how to do our job too. He helps Blount with the HST while I wait outside the radius of the downwash. The two birds disappear and the LZ is quiet again.

I walk over to the inbound cargo area where Johnson has staged the tri-walls with the forklift. I pop open one of the lids to peek inside. It's full of GP tents, rolled up in a pile, as if that's what anyone needs here. Boxes of general purpose tents? The first load we sent out of here was GP tents. Why would we need more? They're olive drab green, not exactly great for concealment in the desert, unless these are meant for the Green Zone, but we don't have anyone living there. There's no ASR number for the tents either, no assault support request. There's no way for us to track where they came from and who sent them, where they're supposed to go exactly. We're expecting other cargo that didn't make it, some fuel bladders, but no dice on that so far. We're supposed to wait up here for another flight later though. Maybe the bladders are coming then. It never matters what I think I know because things are always changing without my knowledge. I get on the radio in one of the Humvees, where I have to reach over the sleeping driver to grab the receiver. I radio to Vargas the cargo we have at the LZ so he can record the info into the official logbook.

"Maybe we're supposed to use these tents to set up a flight line here," Blount yells, peering into the box of tents. "You know, with an office and shit."

"Fuck that," I say. "We're not up here enough and we won't be here forever. Let the next unit deal with it." The small arms fire starts up in the distance again and is joined by the echoes of a Cobra helicopter providing close air support. Johnson usually goes right back in the forklift at the first chance he gets, but instead I see him coming towards me. Then I see two other people walking towards us in the dark. There were no request numbers assigned to any personnel for this flight on the tracker, not that I saw when I checked it in the morning at least.

The two figures introduce themselves as gunnery sergeants from our battalion, from Headquarters Company. Sounds like they're a couple overqualified admin clerks. It makes no sense for them to be here right now. They stare at us in the dark as if they're waiting for us to do a trick for them.

"Corporal Loyette?"

"Right here, Gunnery Sergeant," I say.

"Lance Corporal Vargas?"

"He's back at the FOB," I say. "I have Lance Corporals Johnson and Blount here."

"We've got command climate surveys we need you to fill out, battalion CO's orders. Then we're heading back on the next flight."

So that's it. Our battalion commander is making us fill out surveys in the middle of a war. The random boxes of tents aren't even the weirdest part of our evening. We can hear people shooting at each other a few miles away, and next we know we're sitting cross-legged on the ground with a stubby pencil so we can fill out a bubble sheet. Each of the gunnery sergeants offers to hold a flashlight over our shoulder so we can see the paper. I let Blount and Johnson go first. When it's my turn I sit down and the gunny points a light over my shoulder, and I swear he's got a big smile on his face, but it's hard to see for sure.

"Don't worry, I'm not looking at your responses," he says.

"Thank you, Gunnery Sergeant," I say.

I fill out my survey while the firefight persists in the Green Zone. I fill out my answers to each question as the gunfire and explosions become louder, almost as if the firefight is moving closer to the LZ. I try to focus on the survey. *Circle 1 for strongly disagree, 2 for disagree, 3 for don't know, 4 for agree, and 5 for strongly agree.* The survey is filled with statements such as *My unit is characterized by a high degree of trust.* So, I fill in the circle for my answer: Disagree. *Individuals in my unit are held accountable for their performance.* Don't know. *My CO makes clear what behavior is acceptable and not acceptable in my unit.* Don't know. *Resources in my unit are well managed.* Don't know. *The environment in my unit is characterized by a sense of good order and discipline.* Disagree. *Leaders/supervisors are actively engaged during off-duty hours.* Don't know. How would I know anyway? *My unit provides a safe environment against sexual assault.* Don't know. *My unit would take appropriate action in the case of a hazing investigation.* Don't know. *Members of my unit who consume alcohol do so responsibly.* I answer *Don't know* and I wonder where the hell we would find something to drink around here? All alcohol is prohibited. *Members of my unit who interact with local wildlife do so responsibly.* I answer *Don't know* and I imagine the white dog with porcupine quills in its face. I wonder how we could have been more responsible. Who the hell is going to read these survey responses?

I write down in my ending comments, *I'm filling this out in the dark and there's a firefight going on a couple miles away and this is totally pointless. Have a great day!*

Our names don't go on the survey, so no one will trace the comment back to me. How is any of this normal? Are they pausing the firefight to complete surveys in the Green Zone too? I imagine the Taliban stopping to administer their own paperwork, but I don't mention this comparison to the gunnery sergeants. Bryce didn't tell me all that much about the Marines when he was in. Definitely never talked about shit like this happening. I turn back to the first page and the gunfire stops, not so much as a stray shot after that. The gunnery sergeants gather up the papers and put them in a folder and the silence seems to indicate the firefight is over, unless every single person who participated in it is dead.

The next flight arrives just as we finish. Perfect timing. The two fifty-threes drop off a big rubber fuel bladder, just as we were expecting, and with the ASRs labeled as we expected. The gunnery sergeants get back on one of the birds with our paperwork and that's the last we see of them. The birds each take a net load of the British gear, so we run out and hook them up, which is never pleasant at night. I help in place of Johnson for the second HST. I take a blue chem light out of my dump pouch and crack it so the others can see where I am under the bird. You always use a blue light so the marines know who's in charge. I'm waiting for Blount to ground out the hook so I can secure the net load to the bird. Nothing goes wrong and we get the loads hooked up and then they're gone, and that's it.

"Did that really just happen?" Johnson asks after the birds are gone.

"I think so," I say. "I guess we've seen it all now."

Johnson gets back in the forklift and lifts each fuel bladder into the bed of the Humvees, which nearly buckle under the weight. We don't want to wait for the Humvees to make a round trip, so we hop on back and sit on top of the bladders, resting our boots on the edge of the truck. It's not a safe way to ride on a Humvee. As we bounce down the road, I think about what I would give to be present during the committee meeting that reviews our command climate surveys, the look on the battalion commander's face as someone reads off the data to him. What difference would those responses make to him anyway? It's not like our problems affect his life. No one cares when enlisted people complain. Morale? Yeah, right.

Vargas is waiting for us back at the FOB. We tell him about the surveys and he laughs. What are you supposed to say? He probably thinks we're joking. He gives me the logbook and I check to make sure he's recorded the correct information regarding the fuel bladders we just received, and the tri-walls filled with GP tents. Everything looks fine, so we walk back to our house and drop our gear for the night. I set my flak down and put the logbook on the pedestal, then I realize my daypack isn't in the corner of the main room where I normally leave it.

I find the pack out in the backyard lying on its side by my cot. I approach cautiously because there could be anything nearby, a jackal or a giant porcupine for all I know. But there doesn't appear to be anything. The MRE inside the daypack has been pulled out and opened and everything that was inside is shredded and scattered around. The jackals are smart little fuckers I guess, if they know what's inside an MRE without being able to smell through the sealed packaging. My blue notebook, which I burned, lies in the dirt next to the garbage. But I watched it catch on fire with my own eyes. I pick up the notebook and slide it into the open daypack. When I pick up the daypack I find the spot where it had been sitting is covered in porcupine quills, arranged in a crudely shaped perimeter circle. I pick the quills up in handfuls and toss them over the back wall.

XXVI

The next morning, I grab the green logbook from the pedestal and I slide it into my daypack next to the blue notebook, which I haven't opened yet because I'm afraid to see if new writing has appeared inside. I also don't want the junior marines to see me looking at it or to see that it exists. They know I burned it. I told them I burned it after I saw it burn with my own eyes. I decide to take it with me in case I get a moment of privacy at the COC, then I'll look inside again before burning it in the trash barrel. I need to check in at the COC again to see when the artillery ammunition is scheduled to fly in, if it's scheduled at all yet. The sooner the ammo flies in, the sooner we have one less thing to worry about.

I walk alone across FOB Z and wonder what people expect the experience is like when they think about the war here. Shooting guns, killing bad guys? I always assumed that about my brother. He was infantry after all. Beyond the weird shit going on around here, all that's happened to me is I wake up and go to work, check schedules on a computer, see if anyone emailed me, do HSTs at the LZ, clean, or PT. It's not going to be very exciting to explain my experience to people when I get back home. My brother would have had an easier time telling stories. Combat patrols, detaining persons of interest, calling in airstrikes, shit like that. *I guess I'll just tell people about the dogs here*, I think as I walk into the COC. The front room is empty. I pull up a chair at one of the open computers and log in. I pull out the notebook to look inside since no one's around.

The pages are full of scribbled notes that I don't remember writing. Did I not toss it into the garbage fire like I remember? If that never happened, then I must be going completely crazy. I flip around and look at short passages split up into disconnected paragraphs. I don't know if there's meant to be a pattern as I skim through it. In some cases the words are so messy I can barely read them. It looks like a tree branch grabbed a pen and tried to write a letter. The passages describe things around the FOB, or that's what I can gather as I read through. I can't begin to guess who would've written them:

militia house. the flies come at night. flies in the air. flies on flies. flies on the sleeping marines. marines dream inside. scorpions on the floor. wasps in the dirt. bird's nest, above the doorframe. orange cat and kittens crawl behind the house. dogs crawl behind the house. dogs crawl in the dirt. howling jackals. listen

little corporal and his rank. no one hears him. house of stripes. house of sounds. house of flies. house of face. house of mind. house of wind.

on your own fucking program. he knows, always. roger that. come inside. tell the ma'am. at first, you'll see nothing. at first, you'll see nothing. at

*first, you'll see nothing. at first, you'll see nothing. at
first, you'll see nothing. at first, you'll see nothing.
at first, you'll see nothing. at first, you'll see nothing.
at first, you'll see nothing. at first, you'll see nothing.
at first, you'll see nothing. at first, you'll see nothing.
at first, you'll see nothing. at first, you'll see nothing.
at first, you'll see nothing. at first, you'll see nothing.
at first, you'll see nothing. at first, you'll see nothing.
at first, you'll see nothing. at first, you'll see nothing.
at first, you'll see nothing.*

"I thought the whole point of a diary is you keep it to
your damn self," Staff Sergeant Rynker says, looking over
my shoulder just before I turn the page. *Wow*, I think. *He
snuck up pretty good.* He takes the notebook off the desk
and looks at the page where I left off reading. He grunts to
himself and then laughs. "The militia house. You think you
were all sneaky about it," he says. "I know you went over
there with the Brits. OP Shrine saw you, told us you were
poking around. They see everything that happens from up
there, smart one. And while you're at it, why don't you invite
me next time y'all plan on going for a swim up the road? I
wouldn't mind joinin' ya. It's hot out and I could use a good
swim." He laughs, pauses to shake his head at me. After a
moment he asks, "How old do you think I am?"

"Thirty-five, Staff Sergeant," I say, thinking about the
words in the notebook. Staff Sergeant Rynker doesn't answer
me, so I change my guess and say, "Thirty-three."

"Motherfucker," he says. He rolls my notebook up tight
in his hands. He holds the notebook in front of my face and
widens his eyes. "This trash?" he says. "Is goin' bye-bye. I'm
burning it out back." He laughs and walks back to wherever

it is he spends most of his time all day. He takes one last look at me before he disappears around a corner, laughing and shaking his head. Well, that was easy. I didn't even have to burn it myself, and I certainly would have. It's useless now, full of meaningless notes. I don't need it for anything.

I finally do what I came here to do. I find the updated flight tracker, but there's still no ammo listed on any of the scheduled flights over the next couple days. That figures. When I get back to our house the junior marines are huddled together watching *Billy Madison*, which I can hear playing from Johnson's room on his laptop now that he can finally charge the battery with an adapter. The sound of that movie is unmistakable. I walk into our house quietly, so they don't know I'm there, and I listen to them talking over the audio. But I decide to let them have the time to themselves. I don't need to butt into everything they're doing, and if they're talking about me then I don't want to know what they're saying. I go back to the front room where my main pack is staged and I get ready to go to sleep before their movie is finished, wondering what else Staff Sergeant Rynker might find in the notebook if he reads it before throwing it away.

XXVII

I'm running through the militia house in my dreams again.
The halls fill with smoke from the gunfire. My ears go dead
and start ringing. This time I'm chasing the Soviets. They
fall back to the barracks room upstairs as we fire at them.
Chunks of concrete and plaster chip away and trail through
the hazy air. The stairway is littered with bodies, blood flow-
ing down the steps. We climb over them and move up the
stairs. We storm into the room where they're hiding and
then I'm face-to-face with Blount and Vargas and Johnson,
dressed in Soviet uniforms, and when they look at me I can
see in their eyes that they recognize me. I walk towards them
with a knife in my hand. But then I wake up in my cot. I'm
clenching my teeth inside the mosquito netting under the
moonlight and there's no one there. But there are hands
touching me. Cold fingers caress my face. Something squeezes
my foot, and at that I sit up against the mesh. There's no
one in the backyard with me, just one of the cannons set
up on either side of my cot. I jump when something moves,
a shadow flickering as if someone passes in front of the
moonlight.

"Fuck," I say, my skin tingling where I felt the hands.

I can barely move at first. I climb out of the mosquito net after nothing happens and I carry my rifle with me towards our house. Someone's making noise inside, but Vargas is lying silently on one side of the doorway. He's not whispering. Blount is snoring on the other side, both in their usual spots. I go back out and walk around the side of our house. My boots are silent on the dirt since we cleared out the dead grass and dried-up leaves. I lean close to look through the window until I see Johnson sitting on his cot. His head is in his hands and he's sobbing while trying to stay quiet.

"What the fuck," he whispers. He repeats it a few times and then he lies back on the cot and folds his arms across his chest. He pauses to breathe in and out, as if he had just run a mile. I step away from the window and go to the backyard where my cot sits between the guns. Behind the cot, the silhouette of my daypack is clear in the moonlight. It hangs from a branch. I can't see if it's open or closed. As I get close, I see porcupine quills punched into the ground beneath the daypack in a large shape that opens up and also encircles my cot. The quills had not been there just a few minutes ago.

I look back at our house, but no one's moving. I don't believe any of the junior marines would have done this, or even could have. I can't hear any of the artillery marines moving around next door either. They would be watching to see my reaction if this was a practical joke. I pull all the quills out of the ground and throw them over the wall, then I drag my cot into the house. I guess it really is time for us to move across the FOB to our new barracks. It's probably for the best; it's farther from the militia house. Jackals howl as I carry the cot under my arm. It slams on the floor by accident when I try to set it down in our house, but Vargas and

Blount don't wake up. Maybe they're faking it. Maybe they're really awake. I don't check on them. I lie down and let my mind race, and when I see the drawings on the walls moving, I close my eyes and tell myself it's dark and my mind is playing tricks on me.

XXVIII

The ammunition finally shows up on the tracker and two fifty-threes bring it to the LZ. The pilots fly low over the guardhouse again. This time the guards come down from their houses afterwards, pissed at us because the rotor downwash has thrown a bunch of their shit all over the place and damaged the roof for at least the second or third time. This is an ongoing problem. The Brit pilots never flew directly over the guardhouse in the early days. We have no control over what the pilots do, but the guards getting blasted by wind up there don't know that.

Two men walk down to the LZ, but we don't have an interpreter with us. They work for the same private company as the gate guards along the road. Both of them are carrying loaded AK-47s and are yelling. Corporal Garza climbs out of the first Humvee to help. He manages to intervene and calm the guards down even though no one can understand anything anyone is saying. He looks exhausted as he fake smiles and signals with improvised hand gestures. He looks like he's lost sleep. He buys us enough time to get the howitzer ammunition loaded in the back of a Humvee so we can get out of here. After the two pissed-off guards finally calm down and walk away, we ride back to the FOB.

The artillery marines unload the shells into the house next door as Staff Sergeant Rynker watches. He sees me nearby and he walks up to our house and waves me inside as he enters through the front door. I follow him to the main room where our three cots are arranged around the perimeter and I know exactly what he's going to say. He folds his arms.

"Why's your shit still in here?" he asks and stares at me. "That's not a rhetorical question." Our gear is spread around the room, our helmets and flak vests, main packs, our radio, the logbook, and a pelican case. There's no sign that we're ready to move out like we've been told we're supposed to. It looks like we have no plans to leave.

"I don't know, Staff Sergeant," I say.

"You don't know," says Staff Sergeant Rynker. He suddenly narrows his eyes and points at my daypack, which is unzipped and leaning against the wall. I notice right away that my blue notebook is plainly visible, right inside the main pocket. Staff Sergeant Rynker grunts. I wait for him to accuse me of stealing it from wherever he had been keeping it, but maybe he hadn't been keeping it anywhere. Maybe he tried to burn it too. He pulls the notebook out and flips through the pages, then closes it and puts it back in my daypack. "Keep it if you want it so bad," he says, which surprises me. He glances at the notebook and then he walks towards the front door.

"One more thing," he says. "Your battalion CO got fired and sent home. Heard about it this morning. Not sure what your LT has you clued in on."

"Good to go, Staff Sergeant," I say without reacting. But that's insane news. Our battalion commander getting relieved of command? That's a big deal, the big boss getting fired. I have to confirm this with the lieutenant. Staff Sergeant Rynker looks back one last time.

"Yeah, too bad for him," he says. "Move your shit out of here." Then he's gone. The artillery marines finish situating the ammunition next door. I hear Corporal Garza chewing someone out, but I can't understand the details. Then they leave too and it's quiet again.

I stand over my daypack and I look down at the notebook inside. The cover is good as new, as if it's barely been used. The notebook is full of new writing again. A lot of it is redacted by a black marker. Maybe he didn't mess with it, but he could have. I can see some of the crossed-out words when I hold the pages up to the sunlight, and once again it's not in my handwriting. Too much of it is crossed out for me to read any of the sentences in their complete form. I wish I was done with this. Some of it's in my handwriting. More nonsense about the FOB, descriptions of the scenery and the layout, but not in too much detail that it would violate operational security as if I were writing new blog entries. Then there's a random letter addressed to my sister that mentions Bryce a couple times. No one else could have written this because no one else here knows I had a brother, and no one knows who my sister is or what her name is. I try to keep my family private, even with the lieutenant. The more shit people know about you, the better chance they have of using it against you. I don't talk about Bryce with anyone and I would never write about him, which is just one of the reasons why this makes no sense.

There's a short passage I focus on: *you remember grandma died. mom unloaded the dishwasher. put the dishes away. closed the drawers. but then the drawers were open on their own. all the dishes and silverware on the counter.* A story my mother used to tell us when we were kids after my grandmother died. She used to say the silverware was her mother's way of saying goodbye one last time. I remember her showing me everything laid out on the counter, but I didn't understand what was so important about it then. Hearing the story used to creep me out after that, still does now. I don't like to think of my dead grandmother's ghost wandering around my house when I was a kid. Once again, something no one knows about. No one else could have written it.

I turn more pages but there's no text after that, just a drawing at the bottom of the page resembling the stick figure on the wall in our house. I turn the page and I see it there in the corner of the next page, and the next, and so on. The stick figure appears on the bottom corner of each page like frames in a cartoon, but there's no animation when I flip through, just the same figure standing in the exact same place on each page. Then I flip through the pages a few more times and I get a sense that the stick figure is actually moving, turning its head to look at me, or taking deep breaths. Staff Sergeant Rynker wouldn't be the one to draw stupid pictures like that. I look up from the notebook to see Johnson watching me.

"I think there's something going on," he says.

"Oh yeah?" I say, wanting to say *no shit.* Johnson must have a good reason for bringing this up. He's never wanted to confide in any of us, least of all me. I wonder if something else has happened.

"I have fucked-up dreams," he says. "I didn't before, but I do now. I'm pretty sure you do too."

"How could you know that?" I say. Johnson shakes his

head at the howitzers in the backyard. He's hiding his eyes behind sunglasses.

"There's something going on with Vargas," he says. "He talks in his sleep and I think he gets up at night, like without knowing it. Like sleepwalking. I don't know." Johnson opens his mouth to say more but then stops himself.

"Yeah, I've heard it too," I say. "He told me he prays."

"Prays?" he says. "Do you believe him?"

"I don't know," I say. "But I have heard him doing it since Delaram, whispering in the night, that is. He's always done that, for what it's worth."

"Okay, but what about this?" says Johnson, and then, "Last night I felt hands on me." He looks down at his own hands. "I don't know how to explain it. There wasn't anyone here." He sighs, and I try not to react because I felt the hands too. I don't want the others to overreact, but it's hard to keep my breathing slow and measured as he keeps going. "I think the drawings on the wall move in the dark. You were right about that, but I'm not the one doing it."

"The drawings on the wall," I repeat, and then, "Look. I know this place sucks, but we've only got a few weeks left. We gotta do our job, make shit happen."

"I guess you're right, Corporal," says Johnson. "But what are we supposed to do about everything else?"

"Nothing," I say. "It is what it is." I might as well tell Johnson that the best we can do is get the hell out of here and leave the militia house for someone else to deal with. Johnson walks back inside to gather up his gear and I follow him in to find Blount stuffing things into his main pack. Vargas isn't around.

"You good?" I ask Blount.

"I'm good, Corporal," he says. He doesn't add anything

else, which isn't like him. Blount always has something to say, whether we want to hear it or not. And he doesn't ask me why I'm asking, which also feels off.

"You sure you're good?"

"Yeah," says Blount, then he corrects himself and says, "Yes, Corporal."

I look around for Vargas, but he isn't near our house. I walk across the FOB and I find him outside the COC, reaching into a cardboard box. He doesn't notice me as I approach. I watch him pull out what looks like a newspaper and carry it into the COC with him. Before following him inside, I open the box to find a bundle of *Stars and Stripes* newspapers stacked together. They must have arrived on one of the recent flights. The front cover features a full-size picture of General McChrystal and a headline in all caps that reads BOOTED! I pick up the newspaper and turn to the article.

"Wow," I say. Looks like McChrystal's been relieved of his command of ISAF because he talked too much shit about the president in a *Rolling Stone* interview. I mean, he got fired in public, but they can call it *relieved* if they want. The funny thing is it doesn't matter, because he'll just retire and make six figures for the rest of his life. He'll become an exec or an adviser for some major corporation or he'll make a fortune on the public speaking circuit. Maybe he'll get an official retirement ceremony with a whole formation of troops and an honored guest making speeches about what a great guy he was back when they knew each other at West Point. If what Staff Sergeant Rynker said about our battalion CO was true, then no one's safe from getting shitcanned.

I drop the newspaper in the box and follow Vargas inside the COC. He's sitting in the main computer room, but instead of using a computer he's reading one of the news-papers, like he came here for the purpose of avoiding us. I hesitate in the doorway. What exactly is it that I'm going to ask him, and then what am I supposed to do depending on how he answers the question?

There's no point asking him about weird dreams, talking in his sleep, walking around in the middle of the night because I can't do anything to fix that except to send him away. If I check in with him and find that everything's okay, then I'm the one who's going to seem like I need help. That won't exactly instill more trust in me from his perspective. But if I check in with Vargas and he tells me he's feeling paranoid and having dreams about the militia house, then what? It's not like I could call the lieutenant and tell her I need a replacement for Vargas. He's probably the best marine I have. He does what he's told without asking why, which is exactly what we're supposed to do. Nothing less, nothing more. He makes shit happen, as lance corporals do. It's not like I could go to the battery command and tell them I need a corpsman to examine him because he's having bad dreams. Staff Sergeant Rynker would laugh me out of the room. The only sure way to solve our problems is to leave.

Vargas doesn't notice me standing there. I almost walk out without talking to him, but instead I tap him on the shoulder and say, "Make sure to get your gear packed up so we can move it to the barracks. We need to do that today."

"Aye aye, Corporal," he says.

I figure while I'm here I'll call Delaram and see about this rumor. I pick up a phone and call with Vargas sitting right there; I don't care if he hears any of this. The lieu-tenant answers the phone directly and I ask her about our battalion CO. The lieutenant tells me the rumor is true. Our commanding officer got fired and our new CO is our former battalion XO, the former second-in-command. So that's it. The lieutenant doesn't elaborate other than to say that the decision was taken into account after the command climate surveys were evaluated. There were others relieved along with the CO too, other officers and senior enlisted. None of this really matters from our point of view; it doesn't change what we're responsible for. But it's still crazy to hear.

"Was there anything else?" she asks. "Want me to pass on any messages to anyone else in the platoon?"

"No, ma'am," I say, wondering what messages I would pass. I'm not best friends with anyone in the platoon. "Just wanted to check in and confirm this news." She tells me to stay in touch if we need anything else. She doesn't hint at any departure date for us, which I was secretly hoping for. I don't remind her that she hasn't sent us any Rip Its or Gatorade like she'd originally suggested she would. We say goodbye, then I leave Vargas alone and go out back to the trash fire.

I pull the blue notebook out of my daypack and I tear out the individual pages, rip them in half, crumple them up, tear off the covers until all that's left is a metal spiral with shreds of paper caught in it, and I throw it all into the trash fire. Maybe I've never really burned the notebook, I think, and my mind is just holding on to the false memory of doing it. Things here are getting blurry. I wait near the fire and watch the notebook burn up as I wonder how much longer I'll be alive before I'm in control of at least one aspect of my own life. Fuck it. We'll move our shit out in the morning.

XXIX

I'm asleep and the house is in my head again. I'm watching Blount and Johnson. Both of them are geared up in flaks and Kevlars, carrying their rifles in the dark with magazines loaded. Red flashlight beams flicker across their faces and cut through the blackness around them. They must be somewhere deep down, in whatever kind of basement the stairs lead to. The intonation rings in my ears again, building. I can't hear what they're saying to each other.

Then everything gets fuzzy. Blount and Vargas want to sit on the floor, but there's something wrong with the floor so they don't. I can't see what's on the floor, what's wrong with it. The flashlight isn't pointing directly at it. The floor is covered in something like bones, but it's hard to tell. Small bones, all around, piled together. Then they're both gone. The red moonbeam is sitting where they had once been. Just as I'm about to get a clear look at the bone floor in the dream, I wake up in the silence of our house on the final night we'll sleep here. Blount is lying in his cot but not snoring. Vargas is not in the room. His rifle and gear are staged by his cot.

I find him out back, standing between two of the howitzers in his skivvy shirt and shorts. I figure he's taking a piss, like last time, because his hands are hidden in front of him, so I wait for him to finish. But he doesn't move. A few minutes pass by. He stays still, facing towards the back wall. In fact, he's turned in the direction of the militia house. Not even in a rough estimation; he's facing directly towards it. I get closer and I can hear him whispering the same way he's always doing from his cot. Now I'm close enough to see that his eyes are about half-open. He doesn't react when I wave my hand in front of his face. I lean closer and listen.

"Primero, no verás nada," he says. I wait for a moment to see if he follows up with anything else, maybe something I can understand, considering I don't know Spanish, but he starts to repeat the same thing again. "Primero, no verás nada, y después desearás no—"

I grab his shoulders before he can finish and I shake him once and then hold him steady in case he's really sleepwalking. A wave of energy seems to surge through his body like an electric current. He springs to life and flings a fist out at me, almost hitting my chin, then he stumbles back into one of the howitzers and knocks his head against the barrel.

"Ow," he says, grabbing the barrel to steady himself. He rubs his scalp and groans.

"Holy shit, dude," I say. "Are you okay?" I can't read his facial expression in the dark. I'm afraid to know if he's dreaming about the same things Johnson and I, and probably Blount, have been dreaming about. We don't need any more of this shit in our heads.

"I'm okay, Corporal."

"You were speaking Spanish."

"I was?"

"What were you saying?"

"I don't know."

"Okay, then what were you dreaming about?"

"Dreaming?" he says. "I was just out here making a head call, Corporal."

"No you weren't," I say. "This is what happened last time too, isn't it?"

"Last time?"

"When I found you out here. What's the matter, dude? Do you need to go back to Delaram? We can exchange you with someone else if that's what you need."

"For what? Why would I need to go back?"

"Sleepwalking, obviously. It's not safe here for that."

"I'm not sleepwalking, Corporal."

"Bullshit," I say. "Just like you're not talking in your sleep."

"I don't talk in my sleep."

"What were you just dreaming about?"

"I don't know."

"Yes you do."

"I don't know what it was about," says Vargas, and then, "I don't like my dreams."

"Did you see the stairs when we went to the militia house, the ones leading to a basement?"

He shakes his head.

"Are you sure?" I say.

"Yes."

"I don't know if I believe you," I say. "But fine."

We go back inside and he takes his M16 into his sleeping bag and zips it inside. He looks like he's tucked in, ready for someone to sit on the edge of the cot and tell him a bedtime story now that he's finished with his book. Too bad we don't have any good stories to tell. We have stories, just not any good ones. I lay my rifle on the crossbars beneath my cot, so I can sleep in peace, but I often take it for granted that no one will try to take it from that spot without me knowing, considering how easy it would be to do that.

XXX

In the morning we get everything packed up and ready to carry over to our new barracks near the COC. They want us to move into one room together, all four of us nice and cozy, so we gather everything up. We start heaving it out of our house through the front door just in time for the artillery marines to show up. They walk past our house, right next to the windows, and they gather around the howitzers in the yard. Corporal Garza is with them. He ignores us and shouts orders to his junior marines as they go to work. They rip off the barrel covers and punch in coordinates to make aiming adjustments. From outside I hear someone drop something heavy and then yell *Fuck*, but I don't hear anyone follow up on that. No one shouts for a corpsman. We strap on our gear and carry everything out. I look back to see the gun barrels lift up and point over the back wall. They're about to fire.

It happens just as we turn away from our house to walk towards the opposite end of the FOB. A bunch of marines yell commands from the backyard. Someone shouts *Verified!* And another voice yells *Fire!* An artillery shell blasts from the gun behind us and the air ripples against our skin. The earth shudders and we taste gunpowder. The adrenaline rush causes me to feel focused but also like I'm in a daze. Then the second gun goes off. Then the third. The sound hurts. It's the loudest thing I've ever heard.

They keep firing as we walk. It's everything we've expected. The distance we put between the guns and us has no effect on the sound. It's just as painful once we reach the new barracks, a long building made up of one hallway with rooms on either side. We jump at the sound of the guns as we search for the room. They fire at regular intervals in rhythm, but each sound is just as surprising as the last. We find our room and shut the door. The closed door has almost no muffling effect against the cannon fire. The ceiling shakes. The walls shake.

"We should've just stayed there," Blount says as he drops his gear. He listens and looks up at the single lightbulb on the ceiling that sways back and forth and flickers with each blast. We drop our gear and there's a cramped feeling right away. Four of us packed in here like boots in MOS school.

The walls are plain white. There's a window that's boarded up and sealed off with duct tape. Beneath the window is an AC unit providing the room with foul-smelling air. I kneel in front of it and let the air freeze the sweat on my face, creating a stickiness on my eyelids when I blink. This room was bound to suck. Nothing could be better than having our own house though. But we've all slept in worse places and we can sleep here. It'll do for the next few weeks.

We wait for the firing to stop. It finally does, so we walk back to our house to carry our cots to the barracks. Now the guns are all covered up like they had never been fired today, just like they were set up before we moved out. Everything's the same, but the air still smells like gunpowder. Our busted shower is still standing next to the back wall with the empty black water bag hanging from its hook. Now our house is full of artillery ammunition. They didn't waste any time converting it into a storage shed for explosives. Our cots sit outside the front door in their unfolded position as if someone has tossed them outside in a hurry.

"So that's it," Blount says. He's standing in the doorway, looking at the guns in the backyard. "Back in the barracks again. How many more times are we gonna have to move, dammit?"

"First we'll go back to Delaram," Vargas says. "Then we'll go to Leatherneck. Then to Kyrgyzstan. Then to Lejeune. Then home. Then we'll go back to Lejeune again."

"Okay, I get it," Blount groans as Vargas continues.

"And then we'll go to a treehouse," he says, singing the words as if he were talking to either a baby or a dog. "And then we'll go to a mansion. And then we'll go to the moon. And then we'll go to Disneyland. And then we'll go to the river. And then we'll go to the ocean. And then we'll go to"—he hesitates, and then—"the forest. And then we'll go to the top of a mountain. And then we'll go to the bottom of a mountain. And then we'll go to the militia . . ." He cuts himself off when he notices we're all watching him.

"Let's go," I say.

After we carry our cots back and get situated, we go to evening chow and the four of us sit together. The arty marines seem vaguely happy now that they've finally gotten to shoot off some cannon rounds at real bad guys. I don't overhear anyone talking about whether the mission was a success or not. Corporal Garza sits at the table next to us. Next to him is a junior marine whose skin appears to be a sickly shade of green, who is barely moving, barely chewing the food from this MRE. His cheeks are sunken like that of a mummy and his eyes are barely open. I stop eating at the sight of him and Corporal Garza notices. He laughs and continues chewing as he speaks.

"Oh, don't worry about him," he says. "He just hurt his foot. That's all."

"That dude looked like he was about to die," says Blount as we walk back to the barracks.

"Looked like he was already dead," says Vargas.

I try not to think about it as I brush my teeth in a sink down the hall with running water. I don't want to think about any of us getting injured before we get out of here. We've gotten lucky so far and now we're on the home stretch. Everyone is situated when I return, ready to go to sleep, so I flip off the lights and we try to fall asleep to the sound of the humming air conditioner.

XXXI

Vargas is gone when I wake up. I figure he must have gone to brush his teeth or use the head down the hall. I wait while Johnson and Blount continue sleeping, but Vargas doesn't come back. I get up and pull on my boots without tying them and I walk up and down the barracks hallway. I look through any door that's already open, even if it's only cracked just a little, but I don't see Vargas. I decide to ignore the closed doors for now, because I don't want to piss off the artillery marines trying to sleep. I check out the head, which looks like a warzone. Shards of tile lie sprinkled around the floor like broken glass. Parts of the walls are crumbling or collapsed. This place is a wreck just like everything else. No one's inside the bathroom.

I get back to our room and then see that Vargas's gear is all gone. His flak, helmet, M16, everything. I don't see his day-pack either. This wouldn't matter, but he's been sleepwalking outside, so he could be anywhere. I mean, maybe this isn't him sleepwalking, but there's no flight scheduled today, so there's no reason for him to go anywhere. He's not on the duty roster for back-gate duty, not that I know of. I wonder how often he's been sleepwalking without anyone knowing. Was it Vargas who was fucking with my daypack all those times? Has he been the one fucking with these porcupine quills too? What about the notebook? Blaming Vargas doesn't explain any of those things in a way that would make sense. I just want to find him. I put my cammies on and I leave Blount and Johnson sleeping. I walk across the FOB in order to search our old house, half expecting Vargas to be asleep on the floor in one of the rooms, maybe even curled up next to one of the pallets of artillery rounds.

I don't find him anywhere inside or outside. Then I do notice the stick figure on the wall near the kitchen door. One of its arms is pointing down at something, directly at a line of porcupine quills sticking out of the ground. I wouldn't have noticed if it hadn't been for the drawing's pointing arm, not right away at least. The quills extend from just outside the back door all the way across the yard to the wall, punched into the dirt like fence posts placed at uneven intervals with a sloppy pattern to their arrangement. They alternate between leaning left and right in a weird zigzag, like some kind of demented dinosaur spine dug up by archaeologists. The needles' shadows on the ground are reminiscent of finger bones. If the line were to continue on the other side of the back wall, it would lead to the militia house. The spot at the wall where the line ends is just about where Vargas had been standing when I found him outside the other night when he was facing in the direction of the militia house. I stop by the back gate and I ask the two lance corporals on duty if they've seen a marine walk by or if they've seen anything odd. They look at me like I'm crazy. The militia house sits there in the sun, watching us through the bars of the back gate.

I try my best to block out all the conclusions my mind is jumping to, but I'm in logistics and it's my job to consider worst-case scenarios in order to prevent them from occurring. The worst-case scenario right now is that Vargas is dead or he's in a place where he'll soon be dead. I search the rest of the FOB. Vargas isn't at the chow hall or the COC. He's not at the water tank or the fuel farm. He's not in the staging area near the front gate or up on the hill by the officers' house. I get back to the barracks right as the artillery battery is waking up together and leaving their rooms for morning accountability. I use that chance to walk up and down the hallway once again and confirm that Vargas is not in the building. Now I check all the rooms, even the rooms that were closed earlier. There's nowhere else Vargas could be other than the LZ, but that's a long walk alone. And the gate guards along the road would send him back if he tried to leave, or they would call someone, wouldn't they? There are too many eyes on the front gate for someone to get out alone without being stopped, but OP Shrine also has eyes on the back gate and the militia house at all times, at least when the Royal Marines were here. So why did no one stop Vargas if he went out the back gate? Blount and Johnson are awake when I return to our room.

"Vargas's shit's all gone," Blount says, sitting up on his cot. "Is he on duty?"

I close the door behind me and say, "I don't know where Vargas is. There's no use mincing words. I can't find him anywhere."

"There's only a couple places he could be," says Johnson, who looks from me to Blount to Vargas's cot and then back to me.

"And he's not at any of those places," I say. "Do any of you know about this?" They say no and I ask about Vargas's whispering at night and tell them what he said to me about praying.

"I heard him a couple times when I was trying to go to sleep," says Blount. "I think he was talking in Spanish, so I don't know. Sometimes he did it after reading. Not always. Maybe it's just something he does."

"I don't know," I say. I sit down on my cot and lay my M16 across my lap and I tell them we need to figure this out fast because I can only go so long reporting that my junior marines are all present and accounted for when one of them is missing. That would not go over well during one of the section head meetings. And we don't know if he's safe or not.

"He couldn't just disappear," Johnson says.

"That's not what I said," I say, thinking about what our options are for getting back to the militia house once again. It's the only place I haven't checked. I tell them we need to go find him and I come up with a plan that involves interacting with Staff Sergeant Rynker to a certain degree, which would usually be a last resort but is probably now our only option.

"We can't just wait for him to come back."

"Come back from where?" asks Blount.

"You know where," Johnson says.

"We have to get on the back-gate duty roster and someone has to stay behind," I say, ready to tell Blount he's going with me whether he likes it or not, assuming Johnson will want to stay back anyway. "We need someone at the gate in case the COC does any radio checks."

"I'll go with," says Johnson, then he shakes his head as if regretting it. "Fuck it. Yeah, I guess I will." Blount does not try to change his mind.

"All right," I say. "I'll try to figure this out." I stand up and walk out of our room and I head next door to the COC.

Staff Sergeant Rynker is sitting at one of the office computers when I walk in. He looks over his shoulder to see me out
of the corner of his eye.

"Good morning, Staff Sergeant," I say.

"Good morning," he says, not turning his body the rest of
the way to look at me directly.

"I'm looking to see if I can get my marines on the back-
gate duty roster, Staff Sergeant," I say. "Today if I can."

"Huh?" he says. He lifts his boots over the wooden bench
so he can turn all the way around. He folds his hands across
his lap and looks up at me. "After all that shit from your LT
about y'all being too busy for gate duty, you're telling me you
want to be on the duty roster?"

"I have a junior marine who's getting too lackadaisical and
complacent," I say, trying to use words that appeal to the staff
NCO sensibility. "My junior marines need to get back to the
basics. I told him I would get him on the duty roster today
because he's been slipping." Staff Sergeant Rynker holds out
his palms and then plants his face in them.

"Gate duty is not a damn punishment," he says. "This is
OEF, Devil Dog, not boot camp firewatch."

"I understand, Staff Sergeant, but that's exactly why he
needs to be on duty. I think he needs a reminder that we're
in Afghanistan and not back on the block. Complacency
kills, Staff Sergeant." *Complacency Kills* isn't my invention.
It's the message stamped on the reverse side of the main
entrance sign at Camp Leatherneck. Staff Sergeant Rynker
sighs and sits up straight.

"How old do you think I am?" he says.

"I don't know, Staff Sergeant," I say. "Thirty."

"I'm twenty-seven years old," he says. "I look like I've been
in fifty years after dealing with people like you every step of

the damn way." He shakes his head and takes a close look at me. "You've been losing sleep, Devil. You need to throw that notebook away and get some sleep."

"I threw the notebook away, Staff Sergeant," I say.

"Maybe you did."

"I did, Staff Sergeant. I burned it."

"Well, good for you. *I also* tried to get rid of it. I even tore the pages up myself, Devil, with my own hands." Staff Sergeant Rynker looks at his hands and clears his throat, then he rests his hands on his knees and looks at the floor. He looks up at me once again.

"I read some more of that trash in there too. You think you're so creative," he says and starts laughing. "You write these little stories, but all you're doing is writing what happens to you, like you're the only person here. The lieutenant told me about your writing on the internet, just bitching and moaning about how hard life is, *Oh mommy life as a poge is hard, waaah*. Thank you for your service."

I feel my face getting hot. Staff Sergeant Rynker sees me getting angry and he grins. He sits up straight with his legs spread and his boots planted as if he's about to stand up and get in my face, but he tells me again that I'm not creative, as if he knows what the difference is.

"You think you're the only one here with bad dreams?" asks Staff Sergeant Rynker and then he laughs. "Devil Dog, you're not even the only one of us who's been inside that place. Y'all snuck out like you were on a secret fucking mission. Man, everyone's been over there. I went in with the damn Brits too. They showed us around the first fucking day we were here, which means I was there before you, asshole! And you know what happened at first? Nothing. The Brits told us one of their people went home, trying to say this haunted shit drove him nuts. None of them believe that trash, that's what they told us. Said he was a shitbag. Then we came back out and no one complained about anything because nothing happened. No one started writing love letters in their fucking diaries before you went in there, that's for sure. In fact, nothing happened before y'all went in. Strange, don't you think?"

"I don't know, Staff Sergeant," I say.

"You don't know. Well, that's convenient," he says. "Now I can't get any sleep, not since y'all went in there. I got junior marines, even NCOs sometimes, telling me they have trouble sleeping, that they have dreams, that they hear noises, that stupid pictures pop up on the walls in their rooms. Pictures like the ones I saw in your old house over by the guns, which I find funny, don't you? You know anything about that?"

"No, Staff Sergeant."

"Convenient," he says. "I'd say it's bullshit, but I've seen it too. Shit moving on the walls like you wrote about in your little diary. Fuck all that. What am I supposed to do, Devil? I'm just a staff sergeant. I can't control what's outside of my reach, so no, I'm not putting any of you on duty because that's something I *can* control. I can't fix anything, but I can stop you from fucking it up more. The duty roster is none of your damn business. You're just trying to get close to that place again." He scratches his chin and then asks, "You know what the worst part is?"

"No, Staff Sergeant."

"I care. That's the worst part. That's why I'm stopping you." He points at his own face. "This is a face that cares about you," he says. "I'm a real person, by the way. My name is Dale. You think I reenlisted because someone forced me to? For some reason I keep coming back for more. Somewhere deep down I

must enjoy this shit. Even with fuckers like you. I got nothing against you personally, believe it or not. I just want you
to finish doing your damn job here. Go home and have a few
drinks, get your dick wet, whatever calms you down and keeps
you from running your mouth on the internet about everything that happens here. Good to go?"

"Yes, Staff Sergeant," I say.

"Then get the fuck outta here."

I go back to our room and tell the others that Staff Sergeant Rynker is trying to outsmart us. I want to tell them
we're not the only ones who the militia house is fucking with,
but I don't know what good that does. Makes us feel less
crazy knowing we're not alone? We're still helpless. After we
sit and think a moment, Blount mentions that he has cash in
his wallet and suggests that we could pay off the gate guards
to let us out without saying anything.

"Not like I need cash for anything right now," he says.

"How much?" I ask.

"A hundred. I bet they'd do it for fifty each. I would."

"That's fucking stupid, but probably true," Johnson says.
"And yeah, so would I."

We hash out the rest of it. Blount will stay behind to
watch the PRC-117 in our room just in case the COC needs
to reach us for some reason. If we're not back in one hour,
then he has to tell someone we're missing, most likely Staff
Sergeant Rynker. I don't know if one hour is enough. Two
hours or more feels like too long. We decide it's best to go
in the afternoon, even though any number of things could
happen to Vargas between now and then.

XXXII

Johnson and I fill our CamelBaks and then we gear up and walk over to the back gate. Blount waits in our room with the radio. I don't have a plan for what happens if the guards won't take our bribe money or for what to do if we're gone too long and someone finds out. No one can predict how long it will take us to find Vargas once we're inside. We just have to be quick. We have to try, even without knowing if we'll be inside for five minutes or five days. If we're gone too long we'll get charged with unauthorized absence, but Vargas is more important than any of that bullshit. I keep telling myself he's all that matters. His disappearance has made me suddenly brave. I would be too scared to go back to the militia house if I didn't think he was there.

The two gate guards exchange a skeptical look when we offer them Blount's money to let us out. The first guard takes off his glasses and blows dust off the lenses and puts them back on even though they're just as dirty as before.

"Really?" asks the first guard, looking at his partner again.

"What are you going out there for?" asks the other one.

"We're just looking around," says Johnson.

"You're not fucking with us?"

"No," I say, and they take the money. It's even easier than we thought. They tell us to be back by the time their shift is over in about forty-five minutes. Johnson and I stand by the back gate before passing through. The militia house sits under the sun, surrounded by rocks and dead trees. Wind blows dust across the road as we approach.

"We won't be long," I say as we walk.

"Good to go," says Johnson.

If Vargas isn't inside the militia house, I don't have any more guesses. If he's not in there we'll have to tell the battery command that he's gone, and they'll wonder why we took so long to report it to them. Then we'll get blamed for everything and I guess we'll all burn together. They'll charge us with as many punitive articles as they can.

I glance up at the mountain at OP Shrine as we walk towards the militia house. It was the Brit snipers who had seen us go inside before, so my hope is the new replacements aren't as observant. I have no idea if they're watching us now; they probably are. All they have to do to see us is look down, which is what they spend all day and night doing. I walk a little faster so we can get this over with, and when we reach the militia house I walk right inside without waiting for my eyes to adjust from the light.

I carry my M16 as if it's loaded, like I'm about to pull the trigger. But it's not loaded. I'm not convinced there's anything in here to shoot. My magazines are tucked into their snug pouches mounted on the front of my flak vest, ready to be inserted. I don't expect to use my M16 now, but I'm squeezing it tighter than I ever have.

We walk through the first deck hallway, entering each

room, checking the whole level. I don't bother to call out Vargas's name because if he's in here we will find him. There's nowhere to hide in these rooms. There's nothing in them but garbage and debris left over from the cycles of people like us who come here to shit all over this place and leave with no second thoughts about it. Vargas will either be inside one of the barracks rooms, or not. That's all there is.

We head up to the second deck, and we check each room. Again, no Vargas. I rehearse in my mind what I'll say to Staff Sergeant Rynker. How can I explain that I think Vargas sleepwalked himself off the FOB and disappeared? How could I explain the porcupine quills in our backyard even if he's having dreams too? Maybe he would believe me. Maybe I'll get laughed all the way into a prison cell at Fort Leavenworth. And Vargas will still be missing. Nothing will be solved. I walk out of the last room and head back to the stairs. There's nowhere else to go but back down.

"What are we supposed to do?" asks Johnson from behind me.

Before I can answer him, I reach the first deck to see more steps leading down, the reappearing basement stairs. The walls down there are different, not all shot up with bullet holes, but smooth and pristine. There's no graffiti. Johnson catches up to me and then he notices the stairs and I hear him breathing behind me. I tell Johnson to load a magazine, and I load a magazine into my own rifle and rack the charging handle. Our weapons make loud *click-clack* noises like the guns in action movies. Nothing makes us feel as safe as our guns. I try to slow my breathing but cannot.

"I don't want to go down there," says Johnson. "Fuck."

"Yeah," I say. "But he might be in there." I unclip the moonbeam from my flak and hold it awkwardly in the same hand with my rifle muzzle, then I go first and walk down the stairs deliberately, each step its own individual decision as I wonder how a portion of this building could disappear and reappear at random.

The stairwell descends to a landing that leads around a corner. I take quick ragged breaths as we near the corner, and then we turn and point our rifles at another series of steps leading deeper, down to yet another landing, even darker. We move down and turn the next corner to find a final set of steps that end at an open doorway filled with nothing but pitch black and the smell of a dusty attic. I take more steps down and move closer, holding up my moonbeam in case there's anything to see. I'm about an arm's reach from the doorway when I find a camouflage daypack lying flat on the smooth floor.

XXXIII

We call out to Vargas. Then we wait for an answer. We listen to the silence and we call out again and then we step through the doorway. I go first. I'm unable to see anything inside the room I just entered. It's cool inside. There's nothing moving. I don't hear animals or anything else, no people. I wave the red light around slowly, but the beam doesn't travel far enough to land on anything solid, as if a screen of black smoke is concealing anything beyond just a short distance ahead of me. We could be in a giant room or a small compartment, but we can't see anything to know for sure.

Johnson follows me in. He crouches over the daypack, which is faceup with the shoulder straps tucked underneath as if someone staged it there intentionally. Johnson opens the main zipper while I walk around in circles, trying to find anything else to give me a frame of reference for where we are, hoping my eyes can adjust to the dark and find even a dim source of light somewhere. Maybe I'll run into Vargas or find something else he's dropped, some other clue. I notice behind us the door to the stairwell is difficult to see. There's not much light coming through the threshold.

We're something like two or three floors belowground at this point. I try to keep my body facing towards the door as we search around so I don't lose track.

"Look," Johnson says after emptying Vargas's pack and sifting through the contents. I lean in with my light to see that Johnson has arranged an MRE on the floor next to a tan, fleece beanie. He holds out the green hardcover logbook where we keep track of all the LZ cargo and passengers. Johnson has it opened to the very front page and I can see scribbling in jagged handwriting that overlaps other writing on the page. Why would Vargas take the logbook?

"It's in Spanish," says Johnson, taking a closer look.

"What does it say?"

Johnson looks up at me and says, "How do you know I know Spanish?"

"Oh," I say. "I guess I don't."

"Actually, my Spanish isn't great but it ain't terrible," says Johnson. He pages through the rest of the green logbook before settling on one particular passage. He studies it for a moment. I don't have a great view, but I see the same sentence repeated. Then he closes the logbook and slides it back in the daypack and says, "I think we should go."

"What does it say?"

"Just random creepy shit," says Johnson. "Same thing repeated: primero, no verás nada, y después, desearás no habías visto nada. At first, you'll see nothing, and then you'll wish you saw nothing. Something like that, over and over again."

"Is that what he's been saying in his sleep?" I ask, not remembering what he had been saying out in the backyard the last time I found him.

"I have no idea," says Johnson. He picks up the MRE

and the beanie and stuffs it all back in the daypack before standing up and pulling the straps over his shoulders to carry it with us. He's facing behind me when he says, "Oh fuck."

I turn around and the doorway is gone. I walk towards the general area where we first walked into the basement, or at least the spot where my mind is putting it. I figure I'll bump into a wall or something, but that doesn't happen. The light of my moonbeam doesn't find any doorway or any walls. I've gone past the point where the doorway would have been. Maybe I'm just facing the wrong direction.

"Which way's the door?" I ask.

"It's right where you are."

"No, it's not. I went the wrong way. There's nothing here."

Johnson doesn't respond at first, and then he finally says, "I haven't moved at all. It was right behind me." I tell him to help me find it. We walk in an aimless circle, then we walk in opposite directions and when Johnson's red light starts to fade from sight, I tell him to come back over to me so we don't get separated. I can't lose him too. Then he tells me to wait.

"Listen," he says. I close in on his voice and the red light. When I reach him I don't hear anything at all. What is he talking about? We pause and wait, and Johnson's helmet nods up and down. He lifts an arm and points. I still don't hear anything. If there's really something to hear, then my hearing must be too fucked up from standing underneath helicopters to hear what it is.

"There," he says.

"What is it?" I say. "I've got fucking tinnitus."

"I don't know."

"Well, is it Vargas? Fuck, come on."

"I don't know," says Johnson. I follow him for a bit, but we don't find anything, nor do we encounter any walls or any other rooms or any signs telling us what this place is meant to be. I keep worrying I'll trip over something in the dark, but the floor has been completely flat so far. My red light reaches out in front of me and illuminates the concrete floor in red, but only about five or six feet in front of me. The air is cool, but still. I tell Johnson to stop walking.

"You need to tell me more," I say. "What's going on? What are you hearing? Is it getting louder or not? Give me something to go on."

"I don't know what it is. It's like wind or something," Johnson says. "Or breathing. It's not getting closer, or it is. I can't tell."

"Well shit. I don't feel any wind," I say. I listen again and there's still nothing, no matter how hard I try to hear it, no matter how badly I want to. I tilt my head back and point my light up, but the light doesn't land on any surface, swallowed up by the dark. Where the fuck are we? It seems like it's as big as a gymnasium, maybe even as big as the stadium on campus. That's all I can think to compare it to.

"How far have we walked?" I ask. I want to know if Johnson has an estimate, even if it's not fair for me to keep asking him questions that I don't have an answer for. We stand there and wait in our bubble of red light and Johnson says he thinks we've walked farther than where the edge of the militia house would extend, but there's no way to know for sure.

"It's not that big of a building," he says. "And we've been walking for a while." I want him to be wrong, but he's not. Something terrifying is happening. We can't be directly under the militia house anymore. We physically cannot be. If we were moving towards the river, we would have come out on the side of the slope leading down to the bank. We would be hovering above the Helmand River at this point. In the other direction, we'd be somewhere inside the mountain where the OPs are staged. I don't know. Maybe it's a Soviet bomb shelter that we're lost in, something like that. We're not inside the mountain though. I don't think so. We're somewhere else. It's almost funny now. The rockets and mortars used to scare me at Delaram, the shit the Taliban launched at us. But that feels like years away, like a past life.

XXXIV

My watch reads 15:06. Johnson and I have been walking now for almost an hour. We took too long and now we're stuck, like Arnold warned about. Don't stay too long, he said, and look what we've done. We stop to take a piss, standing back-to-back. We've lost track of each other a few times already. It's too easy. We haven't found any other rooms. Time could be passing at any rate in the outside world, the real world, whatever you want to call it. Things could be going fast or slow and we wouldn't know the difference down here, like we're stuck in some kind of fantasy. I don't say that to Johnson. Maybe we can still find our way out of here before Blount or the gate guards need to tell anyone we're missing. We can't just sit here, no matter what happens.

We clip our moonbeams to the front of our flak vests to keep the light pointed forward and we choose a direction and try to walk in a straight line with the hope of finding a wall, and then hopefully tracing the wall to any other sign of an exit. That's all we got in terms of a plan. There's no sign of Vargas along the way, and I can't hear whatever Johnson says he's hearing. We've agreed that whatever Johnson hears isn't coming from any particular direction, so there's no point in trying to locate the source of it. It feels like we've walked another half mile before I finally tell Johnson to stop walking.

"That's enough for now," I say. I wait and think of what else we could do to figure this out. I don't know. There seems to be no method to anything. Johnson reaches up to his flak vest and unclips a cheap carabiner from the front. I watch him fidget with the carabiner for a bit, turning it over in his fingers. He flings it straight up into the dark above us and then reaches his hands out to catch it. We haven't figured out how high the ceilings are, if that's something important to know. There's no sound of his carabiner hitting a ceiling and it does not fall back into Johnson's open hand. It doesn't fall back to us at all. Johnson pulls the digital camera from a grenade pouch on his flak and turns it on. The digital view-finder screen casts a bluish light onto his face. He points the camera overhead and snaps a picture, the flash flickers out into the room, but the dark swallows the light completely. When Johnson brings the camera close to check the view-finder, I see that the image is a plain black screen, just as it had been when he checked the camera after we first went into the house. But this time there's something else, a cloud of smoke, a smudge on the lens maybe? It's hard to tell. Johnson rubs his thumb across the screen to clear it off, but the smudge remains. Whatever it is in the image, it's right above us. I remember I still have two blue chem lights in the dump pouch on my flak.

"Hold on," I say. I pull one of the chem lights out and rip off the plastic wrap, then I bend it until the inside cracks and the thing lights up blue, which really fucks with my eyes after all the red. This can't be good for our eyes. I fling the chem light straight up and it tumbles end over end. We watch the chem light fall back down to us after it fails to illuminate anything in the air. Johnson picks it up and throws it hard. The blue light spins and lands on the floor where it slides to a stop, so we walk over to pick it up and we take turns throwing it as far as we can.

"Do you hear anything else?" I ask as we walk across the floor to reach the chem light where it last landed.

"Not right now."

Throwing this thing around is a good distraction from whatever's happening down here. It's not a dream. It's real. Vargas is really gone. If we find Vargas, what then? I don't want to interrogate him. I don't care why he came down here. I just want to find him and tell him I'm sorry for being the person who chose to bring him here, as if I had been choosing random names out of a hat for something unimportant. He wouldn't be in this situation if it weren't for me. That goes for all of them. It's my fault they all came to the FOB and to the militia house. Maybe it wasn't all on me that we were brought to Kajaki; that wasn't my decision, but I could have said no when they asked about going to the militia house.

"Why do you think he came down here?" Johnson asks, practically reading my mind as he tosses the blue chem light once more. He stays in front as we walk. Every few steps we take he's been shooting a flash photo with his camera, using the flickers of light to guide us in case anything lies ahead. Each camera flash is worse than the one before, the anticipation building that maybe in one of these instances the light might find something we don't want to find. But we've still found nothing. The floor goes on forever.

"I don't know," I say, which is true, but I also don't want

to talk much. I don't think we should. Maybe Vargas would hear us if we were louder and made ourselves easier for him to find, but if anyone else is down here I don't know if I want them hearing us. If anyone else is down here, they would have been waiting for us before we came, unless there's an entrance we haven't seen yet. I don't want to imagine what kind of person could survive down here, or whatever else might be waiting.

We walk. We walk more. We drink from our CamelBaks, and we stop to piss again. How much longer will our water supply last? There's no water source. There's no source of anything other than the sound that Johnson claims to hear. His camera flashes again and doesn't capture anything. We haven't seen any of those smudges in the image since the first one. I consider that to be a good thing. I worry his battery will die before the camera might be more useful to us later somehow. We'll have to share the MRE and sleep in shifts. We could trade off using the daypack as a pillow I guess, but I'm too keyed up to fall asleep right now. Sleep feels like a trap.

XXXV

Johnson and I take turns lying on the floor and trying to sleep for an hour while the other sits up and keeps watch. An hour is not enough time to fall into a deep enough sleep to dream, at least I hope not. That's the point of the short shifts because it's one of the things I'm worried about right now. If the house can touch you in your dreams even if you're outside it, maybe even control you—which is my only guess as to what happened with Vargas to get him down here—then who knows what happens if you dream while you're inside. We trade off until my watch reads 21:30. They have to know we're not at the FOB by now. Unless time is at a standstill compared to here. I manage to sleep a little, but I wake up sore because we're sleeping on a hard flat surface. We open the MRE from Vargas's pack. The MRE is okay. Johnson takes the peanut butter and I eat the apple cinnamon First Strike Bar, which is dry and chewy but still one of the better snacks you can get in an MRE, even if you're not hungry.

"What if an entire week has gone by out there?" Johnson asks after he squeezes half the peanut butter pack into his mouth. He slurps water from the hose dangling over his shoulder. Each of us has about half a CamelBak's worth of water left. I shrug in the dark, but I doubt he sees me. I crumple up the plastic wrappers after we finish. I'm about to stuff them in the daypack, but instead I toss them away to a random spot on the floor. If we find them again at least we'll know we've been here before. A trail of breadcrumbs of some type would have been helpful from the start, but we didn't know we'd get trapped down here. We didn't know any of this would happen. Johnson asks more questions before I can answer his first.

"How are they gonna know where we are?"

"There's a whole unit up there," I say. "A ton of marines. They have enough people to organize a search. They have to be looking for us."

"How do you know?"

"I don't know anything," I say. "But if a whole week went by, Blount would have to tell them where we were by then. The gate guards too. They wouldn't have a choice. And also, they would flip shit if I missed one of those section meetings they make me go to." Maybe a week has really gone by, but I hope it's only been a few minutes out there. I hope Blount has not had to tell anyone we're gone because by some miracle he's still frozen in the moments shortly after we left. On the other hand, if they know we're missing, Staff Sergeant Rynker probably doesn't need anyone to tell him where we are. But if that keeps things less complicated, then it could be a good thing.

"Maybe it's only been a few minutes out there," I say.

"Well shit, then that means we're gonna fucking starve by the time they find us," says Johnson. He sighs and takes another sip of water. I ask him why he enlisted to get his mind off the situation. I never asked him about that when we were on back-gate duty. I want to keep him talking so he feels something other than despair, but I realize the thought of enlisting might not be the happiest subject. I'm not exactly a therapist though. I don't have a strategy for anything.

"I don't know," he says. "Why did you?"

"I don't know," I say. I think back to the night I was on back-gate duty with him. I was pissed off after our first HST. I still haven't gotten to know him that well since then, which says a lot about me. All of that was over a month ago. Vargas and Blount too, do I know them much better than I did before? It's wild how much time we can spend together without really getting to know each other. I could ask Johnson any other bullshit question at this point, like what his favorite sports team is or what he misses about his hometown or something about his wife, any of that. Instead, I just ask how old he is.

"Twenty-five," he says. "You?"

"Twenty-two."

"Man, I knew you were younger than me."

"How long you been in?"

"A year," says Johnson.

"Only a year?" I say. "Damn, you were an old man when you enlisted." Johnson laughs. He would've been twenty-four, way older than the average age of enlistment.

"What did you do before?" I ask.

"Got married and kept getting laid off from my job. Used to work on cars. Couldn't find another way to pay the bills, so fuck it. Went to boot camp since you get paid from day one. Eventually moved my wife out to Lejeune."

"So you *do* know why you enlisted," I say.

"Guess I do," says Johnson. "What about you then? Anything good?"

"Not really," I say. "I had a brother in the Marines who got blown up in Iraq."

"Shit, and then you joined."

"Yeah," I say, hoping I don't have to be more honest than that, give up too much more. Bryce would have been good at explaining why he enlisted. He would have said he wanted to take control over his own life rather than surrendering to the plans our parents had for us. Ironic, enlisting in the military in order to take control of your life.

"That must have sucked," says Johnson. "I still got my brother."

"Yeah," I say. "It sucked." If I were to say more, I would tell Johnson I never had anything in common with my brother. I was more pissed that he died than I was sad, because it automatically meant that he would be considered a hero, and I would live the rest of my life in the shadow of all the best memories of him recalled by anyone who knew him. Family, friends, anyone. When my brother died it meant I would have to spend the rest of my life trying to be his equal. I could never be better than him. It's too depressing to admit to Johnson. I miss my brother, but it's not as simple as I wish it were.

"Hey, by the way," I say, "back during the HST when the Brits were still here and you were on static for the first time, sorry I pushed you."

"Pushed me?"

"Yeah," I say. "I shoved you when we were under the bird and you fell over. Remember?"

"Wait, you did that on purpose? Damn, I thought the wind knocked you into me by accident."

"Oh shit," I say. "Uh yeah, I meant to push you."

"Good to go," says Johnson. He laughs. "Guess I'll watch my back when you're around."

"Sorry, it's stupid. It was stupid. I don't know what I was thinking. I was pissed off and you were right there. And I don't know what else I would've done; it's not like I'm much bigger than you."

"Man, you're not bigger than me at all."

"Ah geez, all right," I say, laughing. "Fuck off."

We wait for a few minutes. We've been keeping only one of our lights on at a time to conserve the batteries. The single red light keeps us lit just enough to see each other's shape as we sit cross-legged on the floor. The constant red is starting to drive me more than a little crazy. I just want to keep my eyes shut until someone finds us. When I take a closer look at Johnson, I notice he's rocking himself back and forth in place.

"Man, I want to go home," he whispers. He takes in a breath in order to add something else, but then he leaves it at that.

"Where's home?"

"Texas," he says. He laughs and adds, "We're all from Texas."

"I didn't know that," I say, not at all surprised though. A lot of people from Texas join the Marines.

"Yeah," says Johnson.

"All you fuckers from Texas. I've been surrounded this whole time."

"And I can't wait to go back. I'm gonna do *everything*."

I lean back and rest my head on the daypack. It's Johnson's turn to stay awake. I think about what *everything* would mean for me if I got to go home. I make a list in my head that would not seem interesting or adventurous to most people. Take a warm shower. Get drunk. Get laid. Sleep in late. Wear normal clothes. Let my hair grow out and take a break from shaving. Spend all the money I make on the deployment. All the important stuff. It's nice to look forward to something even if thinking about any of that feels foolish right now.

XXXVI

"I hear him," Johnson says. His hands are on my shoulders. I'm lying on the floor not fully awake. "I hear him," he says again. He's standing over me and shaking me. I sit up as he pulls his flak vest over his head, clipping the sides against his waist to keep it secure. He grabs the barrel of his M16 with one hand and heads off with his camera in the other hand. He sets off the camera flash every few steps just as he's been doing when we take our walks, except now he's running.

I call out to Johnson to stop, but he doesn't listen. I lose sight of him quickly. He starts calling Vargas's name, but I don't hear anything other than the sound of Johnson running. No one answers him. I throw on my flak and I gather everything up, the daypack and my Kevlar. He's left his on the floor so I grab that too. I secure the chinstrap on my own helmet and I clip Johnson's helmet onto my flak. Then I try to catch up to him by following the sound of his footsteps and the blinking camera flashes ahead. The sound of my own boots stamping against the floor makes it difficult to hear him, but as I follow Johnson, I finally end up hearing something else. It doesn't sound like a person, but I can't place the sound. Some kind of crackling or crumbling, getting louder. Closer.

"Vargas," Johnson calls out. "We're here, man!" He starts sprinting. Something small and light touches my face as I run, but I can't see what it is at all. Did Johnson throw something at me? It happens again, and then again. I feel it on my sleeves and on my hands. Flies. There's one buzzing at my ear, then another joins it, then another. I hear the drone of them all buzzing together. The camera flash goes off ahead of me, once, twice, three times. The black dots of flies swarm through the air. The camera flashes again, but at an awkward angle, and Johnson cries out in shock. His M16 clatters to the floor. I hear Johnson's body land, but the sound is more like a splash than a thud against a hard surface. I can't tell what's happening, but I watch his red moonbeam twirl through the air and land as if he had thrown it like the chem lights. Johnson's scream is muffled. I sprint the rest of the way towards the red light to find that the floor drops off in front of me.

The concrete floor ends in a straight line. I glimpse the bottom of Johnson's boots resting on the edge of the floor as I close in. They disappear over the edge as he kicks his legs. His screaming trails off as he plummets farther away. I can barely keep my eyes open with the flies swarming at my face, can barely stand there. As I lean closer to what first seems like a cliff, my red moonbeam reveals the drop to be about a foot, leading down to an endless sea of porcupine quills. Johnson's body sinks deeper into them as his muffled cries for help fade off. I can hear him struggling, the quills disturbed as he thrashes around. A basin in the

otherwise flat pile of needles marks the spot where Johnson fell in, sloping down like an antlion's trap. Some of the
individual needles tumble into the center. They click and
crumble together as if they're shifting around and settling
under their own weight. The sound of it echoes up from
deep down. This is what I first heard when I followed him
over here, the crackling noise. The needles smell like the
dirty rooms in the militia house. Old pieces of torn fabric
lie shredded around the surface as if others have fallen in.
Is that it then? Is Johnson gone too?

I reach into my dump pouch and pull out my last chem
light. I crack it and fling it out into the sea of porcupine quills.
While it flips through the air, its light gives no indication of
any ceiling or walls or any boundaries, just like we've gotten
used to. The chem light spins through the black dots of flies
before it lands on the quills. It rests for a moment before it
disappears beneath the surface, pulled under by something
I'm too far away to see. Johnson's M16 lies on the floor next
to his moonbeam and the digital camera with the dim light
of the viewfinder still glowing. You wouldn't know a person
had just been there moments before if not for the things he
dropped. I pick up the camera and put it in one of my grenade
pouches. I kneel down at the edge and take a closer look at
the porcupine quills. They're piled thick. There's no sign of a
floor beneath them. The quills are irregular in size. Some are
as short as a pencil and others maybe a foot long. How could
you rescue someone from that? I don't know who the cloth
shreds belong to, or how long ago those people were here,
but there's no use sticking around to try to figure it out. The
flies gather and I swat them out of my face as I head in the
opposite direction, leaving Johnson behind. I think about
the sea of porcupine quills getting farther away behind me

and I wonder how I will ever be able to fall asleep again for the rest of my life. How could I ever get that image out of my head? Johnson is gone and there's nothing I can do about it. Now I'm completely alone.

XXXVII

Both moonbeams are dead. The camera battery is dead. There's no sign of anyone. Johnson is gone. There's nothing I could have done. I'm trying to accept it. There's no water left. The rest of the MRE has been gone for at least one entire day I think, but I'm not sure. I haven't kept track of everything. At some point I left my helmet behind with my M16. There's no point in carrying either of them. I don't know how far I walked before I decided to stop here. Right now I'm trying to build some energy to walk. All I can do is keep walking. I have my flak laid out on the floor with the daypack emptied and folded in half on top as a cushion to rest my head on. The beanie would be good for extra padding too if it were folded up, but I need to wear it to keep my head warm. I get sore from lying awkwardly on a hard surface, so I sit up to get in a comfortable position. As I open my eyes, the lights come on as if someone has flipped a switch.

I shield my face as if someone is shining a flashlight at me and when I open my eyes to let them adjust, I find my arms resting on the surface of some type of table or desk, a surface with a different texture than the cold basement floor. Then

I notice the sleeves of my shirt. They're not desert MARPAT because I'm not wearing my cammie blouse anymore. I'm wearing a gray hoodie. I'm sitting in some type of fixed chair that can swivel. I'm wearing sweatpants and I've got on flip-flops with no socks as if I had woken up late and just made it in time for class. And then I see the open backpack next to my feet, not a Marine Corps assault pack, but my backpack from school. There's a pen in my hand. There's a notebook on the table in front of me and a line slashed diagonally across the notes on one page as if I crossed something out or had fallen asleep writing mid-sentence and dragged the pen by accident. Then I see that I'm not alone. I'm surrounded by other people.

I'm in a lecture hall and everyone is taking notes. This has to be some kind of dream, right? There's a student scowling at me a few seats away as if me getting my bearings is a distraction to her. She returns her attention to the professor at the front of the room. The professor stands at the bottom of the auditorium-style rows, delivering a lecture to those of us spread out across the tiered seats. The walls and the ceiling are white and the lights cast a yellow hue that makes my eyes ache. The professor paces back and forth behind a podium that sits in front of the stage, but not actually on the stage. The professor approaches a laptop sitting on the podium in order to click to the next slide of the lecture, but I can see from where I'm sitting that his feet are not touching the floor. Is this what happened to Vargas? Did the house send him somewhere else?

I look down at the notes on the page and I can read the words but nothing seems familiar to me. None of it means anything. The professor uses a laser pointer to circle areas on a map with a swirling red dot; the toes of his shoes hover inches from the floor. The map isn't familiar to me. It's not the US or Afghanistan, somewhere else in the world. I don't know what to write, but I keep the pen in my hand and pretend to be writing something. I look around the room, confused. The stale smell of the militia house hasn't gone away. I know I'm still there, even though I'm wearing the real clothes I would have worn to this exact lecture in college, am wearing to this lecture in college right now. This isn't real. It's another dream. I don't know what class this is supposed to be, but I remember this room from campus. Maybe it's western civ, but this isn't the right professor. I haven't thought about any of that in a long time. Boot camp washes a lot of things away. It's like being a kid again, the way your memories seem to start over from the beginning. But this isn't a particular memory from before boot camp and it's not some vision of what things could have been if I didn't drop out of school.

No one is sitting on my immediate right or left. Those chairs are empty, so I have enough space to turn around in my chair without disturbing anyone. I turn and look up the rows behind me and I notice Natalie right away, three or four rows up and sitting off to the side, close to the door. Probably so she can beat the crowd when this class lets out, I think, so she can be on time for her next class in some faraway building across campus. Her schedule was always full like that. Was Natalie even in a class like this with me? That's not how I remember meeting her.

She doesn't see me. She looks up at the professor and then back down at a notebook as she writes. She has a headband pulled over her ears and she hasn't taken her green jacket off. Her cold breath fogs in the air. There is nothing on the projector screen but everyone is writing. I don't understand why

I'm here or what I'm supposed to do. I rest my head on my forearms again to block everything out. If this is where I die, I want it to be quick. I don't want to play these games anymore. I just want it to end.

"What do you fucking want?" I whisper, and then the desk drops out from beneath my arms. Everything drops. I watch the desk and floor, the chair I've been sitting on, the students around me falling like an elevator going down slowly at first, then rushing away. My stomach churns even though I'm not moving at all. The lecture hall below isn't surrounded by the rest of the building or the campus outside; it's not connected to anything else. There's only black. The black encases the light of the lecture hall. There's nothing beyond the perimeter of the room. The lecture hall is a compartment sealed away from everything else, getting smaller until it becomes nothing but a dot of light. I watch it drop between my feet until I can no longer see it. Then I'm suspended alone.

I'm still wearing my casual clothes from the lecture hall. I tip my foot down and my flip-flop should slide off into the abyss, but it doesn't. There's no sense of gravity or weight. I grind my teeth and clench my fists, the pen I'd been taking notes with still gripped in my fingers. There's a feeling like I could fall at any moment but there's no sense of weight or movement. For a while I remain suspended in the dark. None of this can be real, but if it's only a dream then why am I not waking up? I wait and try to control my breathing. Then there's finally the first whisper of a noise, like a draft blowing across an open window, but I still don't feel any wind. I realize the sound is coming from above me.

There's a pinpoint of light in the direction of the sound, similar to the lecture hall as it was disappearing, but now in reverse. The dot grows. It's moving towards me. The sound of roaring wind builds. The light seems far away, but it closes in rapidly and I expect to be subjected to another weird vision. The light expands outward. The boundaries widen from side to side like a horizon. I see features on the surface, a river, mountains. Endless desert. I'm looking down on the landscape of Afghanistan. The sound grows louder until it's a waterfall of white noise blocking out anything else. I see the Kajaki Dam and the LZ, the road. I'm falling towards the FOB and everything about the deployment streams through my mind, all the places and names and the faces of everyone I've worked with and the realization that I truly don't know if there's ever really been a point to any of it other than to keep the cycle going. I think about home. I think about my family and the image of my father flashes into my head. My choice to enlist was just one excuse to not finish college, he told me. I know he was right, I think as I fall. I wonder if the whole reason I ended up here is because I gave up on everything, my life in the real world, whatever potential I had to do good or be a good person, the people who cared about me. As I'm falling, I think about everyone back home. I want them to have closure, but I hope they never learn what really happened to us. I wouldn't wish the truth on anyone. As the ground moves closer, I see the tan, rectangular roof of the militia house, nearly camouflaged with the surrounding desert except for the shadow it casts across the ground. My body is a projectile shooting towards the militia house. I press my eyes shut as it rushes up at me, until I'm close enough to smell the dust.

XXXVIII

Then nothing happens. I'm still lying on the floor, curled up, shivering now. I haven't moved from this spot, not since before the dream. My eyes are open. I'm too afraid to close them, even just to blink. If I close them and open them, I might end up in some other crazy place, another lecture hall again, a shitty dive bar, maybe somewhere worse like the underground sea of porcupine quills that's down here with me, and the torn-up clothes, evidence that someone else might have fallen in before Johnson. That's all there is now. There won't be anything else. I'm not going to find anyone down here. Not even myself. So that's it. I can say I've traveled the world. Now here I am.

I'm not going to find the basement door. I'm not even going to stand back up. I'll just lie here and get used to the feeling of my stomach rattling inside my body, waiting for me to feed it. Then I'll fall asleep. Maybe the militia house will send me somewhere peaceful for the very end. That's all I can hope for. I'm exhausted, but not too exhausted to cry out for a few brief, desperate moments, calling out to Johnson, to Vargas, Staff Sergeant Rynker, anyone. There's no answer, not even from the echo of my own voice. The sound disappears. I call out again.

"Hello?"

This time I hear a dull knocking above, like something bouncing or stomping. I hold my breath. The noise continues as I keep still. There's something breaking through. It must be that. What else could it be? Blount told them where we are, or the gate guards had to admit what happened. A dull, distant crack becomes a sharp crack, and something falls from above and lands on my right calf muscle. The pain shoots up my leg like a rocket. An opening appears above me, a ray of light shining through swirling dust. The light reveals the chunk of ceiling that has landed on my leg.

I lie under the light and I welcome the voices above, and the shadows passing over the hole as people move around outside. I wait to hear Blount's voice. I let it all wash over me. I hear them shouting orders at each other, someone calling out, *I see him; he's down there.* They tell me to look out and they pound against the ceiling from the other side. The material is solid and strong and it takes them forever. More of the ceiling falls in and shatters into brittle pieces, nearly landing on me once more. The light floods in, so bright I can hardly look without feeling a sharp ache in my head. A coil of rope drops through the opening and touches the floor. Several bodies fast-rope down to me, marines in their flaks and helmets, their M16s loaded.

They pull me up onto a stretcher that gets lowered through the opening via rope, my leg throbbing the whole time. One of them notices the injury when I point at it. A corpsman fast-ropes down to help me.

"Got yourself a Purple Heart there," he says offhandedly as he bandages me up.

I try to ask them where Blount is, but I don't think anyone can hear me. I tell them Johnson and Vargas are still here. They strap me down onto the stretcher and I can't focus on what they're saying, it's just a muffled chorus of voices. They strap down my forehead, and then they tighten straps against my wrists. I have the feeling that the pen is still in my hand, the pen from the lecture hall, but I can't bring my hand up to look. There's too much commotion. They're being too loud.

"Where's Blount?" I ask.

They start pulling up the stretcher. My head is strapped in and I can't move it. My lips are as dry as ashes, the inside of my throat stuck to itself like two pieces of fly paper. I see Staff Sergeant Rynker waiting on the surface. He scowls at me with his arms crossed. Blount watches from behind him. I don't see Vargas or Johnson with them. But at least now they know where to look. Things are light and dark. I shift back and forth between wakefulness and deliriousness as they load me into a truck first and then into a Blackhawk helicopter. I question why I'm the one who gets to be so lucky to get rescued. Where's everyone else? I don't understand. I wonder if I will ever get a chance to explain any of this to anyone, and how I would possibly begin to do that.

XXXIX

I'm lying on a bed without knowing how much time has passed. They're telling me I'm not in Kajaki anymore. Different people keep saying it to me, people who circulate in and out of my room, if you can call it a room. I'm in a hospital tent somewhere so they can make sure my leg is all right, that's what they say. My body is injured because of their rescue attempt. That's all the nurse will tell me if I ask anything. He's a Navy officer, some type of lieutenant, whatever they call it on boats. He says my gear is all accounted for and I don't have to worry about that. He comes in and checks on me periodically. Then he leaves and I fall asleep again. I wake back up and he doesn't answer my questions about Vargas and Johnson when I ask him where they are.

"I don't know who they are, Marine," he says. "How would I know that?" He only works in a hospital, he says, not the S2. His job is to take care of me, not keep me informed. I fall asleep again. When I wake up my arm is hooked up to a tube that runs into a clear plastic bag filled with clear fluid. More time goes by before the nurse or the doctor or whoever he is tells me I have a visitor. He steps back out of the room after letting me know. Then I watch the lieutenant walk in. I brace myself for an ass chewing. If I'm supposed to sit up in my bed, sit at the position of attention, I can't move. The lieutenant doesn't seem mad. She walks in and stands next to me.

"Just relax," she says. She looks like she hasn't slept in days.

"Good morning, ma'am," I say. "If it's morning. Is it?

"Don't worry about any of that."

"Do you have any news about Vargas or Johnson?"

"Don't worry about any of that either. We'll get to that eventually."

I fall asleep once more. Then I wake up again and the lieutenant is still there telling me not to worry and she's asking me questions but I can't understand what she means by any of them. She's trying to ask me about the militia house, but it doesn't come out right. Or maybe I'm just imagining that. I can't understand her.

"I'm sorry, ma'am," I say. "I can't understand you." It must be the medicine they've got me on, so I say that. "It must be the medicine," I say.

"Don't worry," she says again. She doesn't seem mad, just tired. She sent us to Kajaki and then all the crazy shit happened on its own, but it must weigh on her still. I can't imagine what any of this is like from her perspective. After all, anything that happens to her marines is her responsibility. I used to think I could do her job, but maybe I was wrong. I want to know what she knows, but I don't want to be in her shoes. I want to know if they're searching for Vargas and Johnson or if they've already been found and if so whether or not they're okay. What's being done about it? Instead, the lieutenant tells me I'm going home. They're sending me home early.

I'm going home early to recover, she says. The rest of the platoon will remain in-country and stick to their routines until proper relief arrives. They'll just be doing it all without me. The battalion will start looking into everything else once we get back to Lejeune and everyone is fully demobilized. She tells me I'm not to discuss any of this with anyone, as it's all classified and under investigation. She tells me I'm lucky I'm not being detained by NCIS right off the bat because if I wasn't injured that's what would most likely have happened. That's the standard procedure.

"I'm not saying that to scare you," she says. "That's just how things are. That's how it works." She waits next to my hospital bed, but I don't know what else there is for either of us to say.

I get to go home early, but what makes me so special? If I get to go home early then everyone should get to go home early. When I ask about Blount, the lieutenant says, "I told you not to worry about them." I have trouble remembering earlier parts of the conversation. She says I'm not to try to contact anyone in the platoon while I'm home, says I should enjoy my time out of uniform, try to relax, but keep a phone nearby in case anyone needs to check in with me. Don't leave my hometown. They need to know where I am at all times. She reminds me the last thing I want to do while I'm at home is to get myself into more trouble.

"How did they find me?" I ask. I'm dying to know something, anything. Even the smallest detail. I've spent my entire enlisted career being kept in the dark, only ever knowing what someone else thinks I need to know. She says they found me because they looked in the only place left where I could have been. She says I shouldn't be worried.

"Blount did the right thing," she says. "He helped us."

"I saw Johnson disappear," I say. I go through the whole thing, how Johnson was running and then he fell into a pile of giant porcupine quills and disappeared beneath the surface as if he'd been drowning in a body of water. The lieutenant looks at me like I'm speaking another language. I tell her everything, going all the way back to the night when we first saw the dog at the back gate. I eventually stop talking. The lieutenant opens her mouth to respond, then hesitates. She finally speaks.

"It doesn't sound like any of that really happened, Corporal," she says. "I'll be honest. I don't believe you. Frankly, it sounds like something you might post on the internet."

Unbelievable, I think. It hurts for someone who I respect to assume my only motivation is to get attention from posting shit on the internet. Writing blogs isn't something I care about as much as everyone seems to think. In fact, it's not something I care about at all. It was just something to do. Something to look forward to after a long day on the flight line. Just part of a routine.

"Where's Blount, ma'am?" I ask.

"He'll be fine," she says. "Don't worry about any of that. By this time next week, you'll be home and you won't have to worry about anything for a while. For now, it's my job to do the worrying."

XL

My flight back to the States is full of Army guys. We take off from Kyrgyzstan and land in Romania. I'm wearing my desert MARPAT uniform, which is filthy. You're not allowed to wear it off base under normal circumstances, but it's all the clothing I have. They sent the rest of my gear and belongings back to Lejeune. Everyone on this flight is returning home to their families under typical circumstances, except me. They've all completed their deployments and done their jobs and now it's someone else's turn to take over in their place. For them, things are happening as they're expected to happen. I'm still covered in dust.

My leg feels a lot better now as I walk with only a slight limp up to the counter at an airport bar. I buy a cold beer in a green bottle, some European brand I've never heard of. I don't look closely at the label, but something about the green bottle makes it seem more appealing, makes me feel thirsty. The Army CO tells his people their drink limit is two drinks per person at each airport layover, but I'm not in the Army, so his little pep talk is merely noise. I don't listen. I don't think any of them are about to bother me. Why would they? They're ready to go home and take some leave, tell a bunch of stories about their deployment. None of the people in charge have tried to keep track of me. They've mostly ignored me so far.

I take the cold bottle of beer and walk over to a bench in the crowded terminal. I sit down next to a man and woman, a younger couple. It's been so long since I've been around normal people. They ask me some questions in broken English. I assume they're Romanian because we're in Romania. They thank me for my service for some reason. Maybe they think saying *Thank you for your service* is just an American way to greet people wearing uniforms. Otherwise, what do they care? I haven't done anything to improve their lives. I'm not the one keeping this place safe. There are guards walking around the airport doing that, wearing tactical gear, carrying submachine guns loaded with high-capacity magazines. Why doesn't the Romanian couple say thank you to them? They get up to catch their flight and I walk around the terminal and watch the soldiers from my flight spend money on souvenirs.

After a second beer, I'm already buzzing hard. I haven't had a drop in nearly seven months. I stumble my way back onto the plane, dizzy. We fly to Leipzig next. I drink more beer in the airport and I wander around there too, trying not to bump into anyone. The soldiers buy one-ounce bottles of absinthe and after a few of them complain of not seeing a little green man standing on the bottle, I offer to drink the rest for them. I take one of the bottles and pour the liquor down my throat and it's so bad I almost spit it out. It doesn't taste like what I was hoping it would taste like and I don't hallucinate a green man either.

We get back on the plane. I let the hum of the engines

pull me away and I dream about the desert. The desert is an ocean floor. The militia house appears from the shadows, debris floating around it as I drift closer. The plane shudders, jogging me awake. I'm grateful it has done so.

XLI

My cammies are still covered in dust when I step into the terminal and I still smell like shit. I'm drunk when I step off the plane to meet my family. It doesn't feel right coming back alone, leaving the others in the platoon behind, but I can't be sober thinking about that shit right now, so I'm glad I'm drunk; otherwise I'll get lost in my own head. The terminal is crowded, but I see my family right away. I spot my parents and my sister waiting with a sign, it has a red background with gold letters reading WELCOME HOME ALEX. I join them and the four of us embrace in a hug while everyone in the airport stares at us like there's some kind of fairy-tale happy ending unfolding in front of them. It's weird seeing my family for the first time in so long, especially when I haven't talked to any of them since we had prepaid phone cards at Delaram. It's been months since then. Random people approach and reach out to shake my hand, thanking me for something so they can feel better about their own lives. Some guy says in a shaky voice like he's about to cry, "Thank you . . . for everything." Would they thank me if they knew that all I did was fuck around with cargo at the LZ?

Would they thank me after watching us hook an external load? All I do is boring shit. I'm just a poge. They wouldn't be impressed if they knew what that was.

"How does it feel to be back?" asks my mother. Her hand is rubbing the side of my arm, even though the fabric is encrusted with dried sweat. She smiles at me but it feels like an unsure smile as if she doesn't know what my voice is going to sound like. This is my family's first chance to welcome home a son like this, but it should be the second.

"It feels weird, but good," I say. "Really good to see you." My family looks at me like they're looking at a ghost. Claire hugs me again. I'm pretty sure she made the sign. "Could you fold that up?" I ask, so Claire folds up the sign and I feel bad for making her do it. It's just that I don't want to draw a bunch of unnecessary attention to myself. No one needs to throw a party for me. I'm not proud of anything enough to celebrate it.

"Here you go, bud," my father says. He hands me a duffel bag and says there's some clean clothes in it, so I walk through the crowd to find a bathroom and there are so many people wandering around aimlessly in the airport, the most people I've seen packed into the same place in a long time. I didn't know what to expect upon seeing my family again, but I'm glad they knew I would need clean clothes. Whoever told them I was coming must have mentioned it, the lieutenant maybe if it wasn't a communication from the Red Cross or the battalion family readiness officer.

I walk into a bathroom and all these guys are nodding at me with a solemn look on their faces like they were already expecting me to show up in this place at this exact time. I guess they approve of something they see, probably the uniform. One of the things you don't expect about the military is how hard it is to blend in while wearing camouflage. I track dust all over the floor as I walk across the room to a bathroom stall.

When I open the duffel bag I find a T-shirt and a pair of jeans that look like they came straight from being stuffed inside one of my dresser drawers, all wrinkled to hell, just how I would have left them before we shipped out on the deployment. There's a pair of tennis shoes and I can't get my boots off fast enough. My shoulder bumps against the wall. Regular-people shoes, I think. They feel wonderful.

There are so many firsts occurring right now. The first time in months I'm standing in a normal bathroom that isn't a wooden shack, a porta john filled with flies, one of those modified shipping containers with the sinks and showers in it, or just an old dirty toilet seat nailed to a wooden board. First time seeing my own reflection in a mirror that isn't one of those shitty blue shave-mirrors they put on the packing list. First time putting on a dry, soft pair of clean socks since before we made it to Kajaki, back when we had real laundry machines and not just buckets of brown water, powdered detergent, and soiled scuzz brushes. First time thinking of myself as just Alex and not as *Corporal Loyette*.

I walk out of the bathroom and Claire can't help but to latch back onto me once again. I hug her back with my free arm. She's still in high school. She just got her driver's license. She only has one older brother left. I'm so scrambled up with emotions I don't know which is the right one to focus on first, so for now I surrender to the joy. I'm happy for my sister and my parents, that I'm able to return to them alive. And I'm happy for myself too, to be with the people who care about me as a person rather than as an asset. I feel lucky, even if there's guilt to go along with it when I remember why

I'm here. I left people behind, but I'm happy to be home. I can't help it.

My mother and father look how people look when you haven't seen them in years, which is partly what you expect, I guess, that people change when you don't see them for a while. People get older. It's almost like I forgot what they look like. They don't say anything about Afghanistan. I don't know how to read them. It's fine, because I don't really want to be asked anything about Afghanistan right now. Every TV in the terminal is playing CNN and it looks like there's something on the air about McChrystal getting relieved of his command. It's a big deal. Our battalion CO getting relieved is a big deal too, but McChrystal is practically a public figure. I imagine everyone asking me for all my opinions and philosophies about the war now that I've been *over there*. I'll be expected to know everything and answer for everything, even though the war started when I was a kid. All I can think about is the militia house, but there's no way I can talk about any of that with anyone.

We walk out of the terminal and across the parking lot to the car, another first: riding in a vehicle designed for comfort in favor of pure efficiency. I sit in the front passenger seat and recline it back a little bit, stretching out my legs and closing my eyes. A seat like this would have made the convoy I went on much better. After a while, my mother asks if there's anything special I want to do while I'm back home but I pretend I'm asleep and don't answer. She keeps talking to me though, saying she's so glad to have me home no matter how long I'll be back. She says I could spend all day and night sleeping and she would just be happy to know I was in the house. That's what she says. My father and Claire don't say anything in the back. I feel bad for ignoring them, but then I fall asleep for real. When I wake up, we're in the driveway and it's a huge relief to be home.

I carry the duffel bag into the house and go straight upstairs into my bedroom and it's like no one has touched my room since before I went to boot camp, just like Bryce's room, except my door isn't locked. My door is wide open, ready for me to walk in. Everything is still in place, the faded baseball posters taped up around the room and the stupid boot camp headshot of me in dress blues hanging in a frame. I want to take that picture and put it facedown in a drawer somewhere. Maybe I can just give it back to my parents to keep for themselves. I'm bitter, but I shouldn't let people know that. The last thing I want now is for people to be uncomfortable around me like I'm some kind of beast, presuming I'm going to blow my top if they say the wrong thing in front of me. It's funny because that's probably what I really wanted when I first enlisted, for everyone to see me as a tough guy like that. Back then, I wanted everyone to leave me alone.

The black pelican case I mailed home midway through the deployment is locked in the corner of the room, full of gear I didn't need then and don't need now. I leave it locked and I reactivate my cell phone service. I text my friend Tyler, who still lives in town, the one friend who's usually down to hang out on short notice because he doesn't have anything else going on. He's always in search of the next epic night out. I figure he'll want to know I'm back in town. I'm still kind of drunk and I want to drink more. Maybe Tyler can help me out with that. I send out a text message saying I'm back in town, asking what he's up to and if he wants to meet up. In the meantime, I drop the phone on my bed and head to the bathroom to have my first real shower in months.

The hot water coats my arms and legs in warmth and I almost crumple to the bathtub floor in ecstasy. The layer of Afghanistan dirt gathers at my feet in a brown puddle before swirling down the drain. This is even better than I could have imagined. I stay in the shower longer than I should, much longer than the drill instructors teach you to in boot camp. I convince myself I'm doing it for all the marines still in Kajaki, as if they would be so grateful to know that my first shower in the States was in their honor. They would probably tell me to fuck off. The shower feels that much better when I imagine the FOB. I let the hot water flow over my forehead and down my chin, wondering what's next, whether it will be good or bad or anything in between.

XLII

I lie awake in my bed after I don't get a text back from Tyler. I try not to fall asleep because I'm still afraid to dream about anything. I don't want to see the dog or Johnson in my head. I don't want to imagine the emptiness. I'm living all of these separate lives and none of them are intersecting right now and it's making me feel crazy as my mind races. I'm in a different world, a whole universe away from the one where we went inside the militia house, different than the universe where we went to Afghanistan at all. Everything around me is totally removed. There's not a trace of anything here. The war's still going on, but I'm here. How do I reconcile that? Everything here looks different and sounds different and smells different. There's no guns or tanks or bombs. What does it mean? What am I supposed to do? I check my cell phone and the time reads 02:24.

I sneak out of my bedroom and try to open the door slowly to keep the hinges from creaking. Shit, in Afghanistan we didn't even have doors most of the time. The stairs leading to the first floor are creaky, as are the stairs leading from the kitchen down to the basement. It's like the house makes an audible response each time I move. I end up at the family desktop computer in the basement, and I log in with my old account info from before I first moved out of the house. It still works. When I get signed in, I log on to my MOL account. Posted next to the two medals I had originally been awarded—the National Defense Medal and the GWOT Service Medal—are three new awards: the Sea Service Deployment Ribbon, the NATO ISAF Medal, and the Afghanistan Campaign Medal. Even if we tried to forget all of this, I'll have everything pinned to my chest as a reminder, an eighth of an inch above my left breast pocket, centered, for the rest of my life.

XLIII

Birds chirp outside my window in the morning. There's no reason to get out of bed, so I don't. It's an odd feeling to be without an appointed place of duty, like the feeling of being without my rifle. Now I carry a cell phone. I forget it's there until I turn to my side and see it on the end table. I've been without it for half the year. It's a foreign object to me. Looks like Tyler finally responded to my text. He seems pretty excited to hang out later. The text reads, *yea bro lets get fuckd up. welcome home!* It will at least be nice to get my mind off everything. He suggests a bar in town that hosts a guy who plays piano. Apparently the drinks are cheap and he takes just about any song request you have for him. So I type out, *roger that*, and hit send. Roger that. The phrase reminds me of Nicki Minaj. Maybe I'll have Claire drive me out somewhere so I can get one of her CDs. She's at school all day today.

I turn my phone off and sleep the rest of the morning and part of the early afternoon. When I wake up I'm so hungry I eat five bowls of cereal. My parents are still gone at work. I text Tyler but he's probably at work too, whatever that means these days. I have no idea what he does for a living now. As I rinse out the cereal bowl in the kitchen sink, I think about what I was doing last week on this day. Enough time has passed since we left the FOB to search for Vargas that it feels like a lifetime ago. It feels far away, but the itch between my toes flares up to remind me it hasn't been long.

I walk downstairs and outside to the backyard, where I pace around in the grass. Everyone is gone. Couldn't they have taken a day off? I don't need to be smothered, but it's weird that no one stayed home. I go back inside and I sleep until after lunchtime, then Tyler comes to pick me up from the house. I feel bad for leaving before anyone gets home, but it's not like they made the time for me. It's not like me being home is a surprise to them. They knew I was coming. They expect me to be here when they get back, but they can't expect me to sit around and wait for them to be available. I need to get out of here and do something, be purposeful in some way. Maybe my family doesn't understand that. You just have to be patient with people. No one here has experienced the desert. They don't know what it's like to walk out back at night and find a pile of porcupine quills.

"What's up?" I say when I climb into the passenger seat.

"Dude," he says. "It's crazy to see you." He reaches out to fist-bump me. He looks exactly how I remember, and I try to think of when I would have seen him last, but I don't know. He was a good friend growing up, but now he's one of those people you run into when you're back in your hometown. I suggest a local barbecue place on the west side of town that we used to frequent back in high school.

"Roger that," says Tyler. He shifts the car into drive and we make it there in less than ten minutes. I tell him we should eat inside, because I don't want to take the food to whatever shithole he's currently living in. I also feel compelled to go inside as a rule. The walls and ceilings feel secure and safe. When I'm inside, I can see the routes that anyone could take to get in and out of a room. I can make a plan for entering and exiting. I can predict the future. The same can't be said outdoors, where there are too many variables, too many open spaces and opportunities.

"How do you feel?" asks Tyler after we get our food and sit down.

"Weird, but good," I say. "Like I'm kind of on vacation." That part is mostly true, but I feel nervous to go back to Camp Lejeune when the battalion returns from the deployment. I don't know what it's going to be like. How many hearings and interrogations am I going to have to sit through? Vacations should be relaxing, but this one is filled with anticipation. The pulled pork doesn't taste as good as I was imagining it would, but it's still not bad. I try to remember to take nothing for granted. I walk to the front counter when we finish eating and I order another sandwich. I'm used to eating MREs, so I could probably make room for a third, maybe a fourth. Tyler watches me eat. I don't feel good when I finish, but not because I'm too full. I'm too embarrassed to admit that I'm still hungry. I suggest we go back to Tyler's apartment now that we're done eating, so we walk back to his car and drive across town to his apartment. The place is a mess, just like I predicted. It's a small one-bedroom place that's cluttered and sparsely decorated. There's a small fake Christmas tree on top of a bookshelf in the corner that I'm not sure if he has put out too early or just never took down from the year prior.

"So, what's it like overseas?" he asks as we sit on his couch. He holds out a translucent glass pipe packed with marijuana that has been sitting on the coffee table.

"I can't smoke," I say, waving it away, not that I really want any to begin with. I hate pot, but I don't tell him that. I add, "Piss test is probably the first thing they'll do when I get back."

"Oh, my bad," Tyler says.

"It sucks, to answer your question," I say as he flicks his thumb across a lighter and holds the flame to the pipe. The marijuana glows orange as he breathes in and then blows out a cloud of smoke towards the ceiling. The room immediately smells like a dead animal and I try not to visibly gag because I don't want to offend him or anything. Pot has always smelled awful to me, but this is worse somehow.

"Yeah. I read your blog," Tyler says, continuing as he smokes more. "It was depressing. I mean it was good, I don't mean to say it wasn't good, but it was depressing. Sounds like things aren't that great. What happened to it, by the way? I tried to find it a few weeks ago to show a friend of mine, but it was gone."

"Wasn't worth keeping online," I say, and then before he asks why, I say, "It was too depressing." If I tell him the whole story about all that, then I'll have to explain everything involving the concept of operational security and beyond, which I don't feel like getting into. So I decide to save that story for another time or maybe never.

"I see," says Tyler.

I manage to keep it together for a while as we play some video games, even though I'm still hungry and the apartment smells terrible. We finally leave to get to the bar around seven. I've been expecting someone from my family to call and see where I am, but I still haven't heard from them. We walk in and the piano guy isn't playing yet, but the Long Islands are only a couple bucks, so Tyler gets us a round of two each. The drinks come in small plastic cups. We drink them fast because they're sweet and also because they're mostly ice.

We sit at the bar and don't really say much because of the hard rock blasting through the overhead speakers. The room is dimly lit, making it difficult to keep track of the people sitting in the shadowy corners. I've never been inside this place before. The outside of the building always looked like it was made of sheet metal and I had assumed until now that it was a barn or a garage. I guess it's weird how certain expectations are not met. Tyler tells me the main concert venue where the piano guy plays is in a separate room next to the shabby bar area in the front.

We finish each of our first two drinks and I offer to buy the next round but Tyler waves me off and says he's not done welcoming me home yet. He seems kind of fucked up already the way he's laughing a lot more now than he was earlier. He laughs at everything I say. More people filter in and I expect to run into everyone from high school who I tend to run into when I'm home on leave, the people who never seem to do anything different with their lives. People like Tyler, I guess. Surprisingly, as the place fills up, I don't end up seeing any familiar faces. Tyler and I walk into the next room, which is dark and wide open with a stage in the front. There's way more space in here than it looks from the outside.

Then there's a guy who walks across the stage and sits at a piano. He starts playing and a funny thing happens. We're in a large, dark room and it's difficult to tell who I'm looking at until I'm right in front of them. People are facing all different directions, walking around, some of them dancing, others just trying to squeeze past me in the crowd. I lose sight of Tyler for a moment, then it starts to feel like every direction I turn I end up accidentally staring at someone without meaning to. At least it's dark enough for people not to see how awkward I am. There's a vulnerable feeling to being part of the crowd, even though crowds feel safe. I'm enclosed within the group, but I'm also out in the open.

When the piano player isn't drowning out the other noise, the crowd is loud enough to throw off my concentration. I feel like I'm the only one in the room who doesn't know the words to every song. Everyone is singing along. Nothing sounds familiar. Did I just forget? I haven't been away all that long. I admit to myself that I'm not enjoying any of this. I haven't been since we first walked in.

I finish the Long Island and I drop the cold, ice-filled cup into a trash can. I start pushing through people who don't seem to notice me even though I get the feeling that everyone is watching. I'm blending in with everyone and I'm the center of attention. I bump into Tyler and I want to tell him I need to go take a piss instead of being honest and telling him I just need to get the fuck out of here. I put my hand on his shoulder to pull him close and then my hand isn't on his shoulder, it's on the shoulder of the crew chief of a CH-53 and we're standing out in the dust.

The crew chief's face glows blue from my chem light. I'm squinting to keep the dirt out of my eyes and I'm yelling into his ear because we can barely hear each other's voices over the roar of the helicopter engines. The bird sits across the LZ from us, the rotor blurred by the constant spinning motion. The image hits me like a wall. I don't know what I yell into Tyler's ear.

"What," he shouts back.

"I said I'll be back," I yell. He's still making a face like he's trying to understand what I'm saying so I just smile and nod to emphasize that everything is okay regardless of whether or not it really is. Tyler smiles back so I assume he gets the picture. I think he tells me to get him another round. I'm sure he won't complain if I bring back more drinks, even if that isn't what he asked for.

I use the bathroom and shove my way to the bar after that. I buy four more Long Islands but I don't want to bring them back into the main room because I don't know who to look at or how to talk to anyone or how to look like I'm having fun. I just want to disappear back into a place I've been hoping to get away from. I drink my two Long Islands to help, and then I carry the other two in each hand on my way to give them to Tyler, the freezing mixture spilling over my wrists and fingers as I'm nudged and pushed by the people surrounding me in the dark. Lights flash against Natalie's face in the crowd, but when I move towards her, she's gone. Wait. Natalie? Where did she come from? I call her name but people are closing in around me and I can't push through their shoulders. It wouldn't make sense for her to be here. I must really be drunk.

The next thing I know I'm outside and Tyler and Claire are on either side of me, holding me up on the sidewalk, and I'm drunkenly shouting swear words across the street at some stranger who's also drunk. When did Claire get here? She wasn't here at first. Did Tyler call her to come pick me up?

"When did you get here?" I ask. "Did Tyler call you? Are you his backup?"

"You better not wake up Mom and Dad when we get home," she says. She has my left arm slung over her shoulder, my wrist tightly in her grasp, but I manage to pull my arm away from her and get my hand into my pocket. Tyler tries to keep pulling me along, but I open my wallet up and start taking everything out one at a time, the cash inside, my driver's license, debit card, military ID, Tricare insurance card, my old college ID, which is still in my wallet for some reason. How did that get there? I throw them at the street, aiming for the gutter. I take each item and fling it from between my fingers.

"Oh my God," Claire yells. "What are you doing?" She runs around, struggling to pick up each of the items from my wallet. Tyler snatches the wallet from my hand while I laugh. I lose my balance and fall to the ground, continuing to laugh even though I get mud smeared all over my clothes. Tyler shrugs and doesn't offer to help me up. I guess none of this is fun for him anymore either.

I deserve to get covered in mud. I think about Afghanistan and I drunk cry. I think about the twelve-hour shifts we worked on the flight line at Leatherneck, and how I've gone from that, to getting promoted, to being a mess on the sidewalk outside some trashy dive bar in my hometown. I think about how I've actually lost two of the people I was assigned to take care of and not just the original one we went looking for. I vomit on the sidewalk under the orange-yellow glow of a streetlamp. Then I wallow in my own pathetic sorrow as my childhood friend and my little sister carry me home.

XLIV

My head throbs the next morning. A ray of sunlight burns through the window against my sweaty face. Both of my feet are lying flat on the bedroom floor as if I had been sitting on the edge of my bed the moment I passed out, whenever that was. I don't remember Tyler and Claire bringing me in here. With my low tolerance it doesn't take much for me to black out. I hear some footsteps and then see my mother standing outside the door.

"Good morning," she says. "Feeling all right?"

"Yeah," I say. I quickly move my feet from the floor to my bed as if I've been intending to keep my shoes on all along. The motion causes a surge in my stomach, but not as if something toxic is churning up inside me. More like an uncomfortable emptiness reaching up through my throat. I feel like I might burp or heave, so I hold still for a moment to let the sensation pass. I look at my phone and there's only one text that reads, *hope your still alive*, from Tyler. He deserves some credit. He didn't pry too much about Afghanistan and he's part of the reason I'm home safe. He never asked me if I killed anyone, which is a good start. I figure I should probably call him at some point and apologize for last night, or at least offer to buy him a case of beer to make up for it. I'll think about it at least. I don't want to admit I'm wrong, but maybe that's the only way to feel like I resolved the situation.

My mother is still standing in the doorway. "Why don't you come outside," she says as she disappears from view. "Get some fresh air. It's nice out."

I sigh and then I get up. I feel like shit and I'm not in the mood to hear any life lessons if that's what she has in store for me. I follow her downstairs and then out the patio door and into the backyard. She leads me over to a coiled-up hose mounted on the side of our house. Wire frames stand next to the wall with green stalks and leaves reaching out from within, a vegetable garden growing strong through the summer.

"What do you think?" she asks. She opens her arms at the plants as if their leaves are radiating energy that she's now absorbing. My mother is a part-time manager at a local craft store in town, so I guess she's off work today and I feel bad she's stuck here with me because all I want to do is go back to sleep. Blacking out at the piano bar is just another thing to feel guilty about.

"Cool," I say. The middle plant holds eight small tomatoes arranged in a symmetrical, rectangular cluster. That's pretty neat, I think, but I don't want to have to talk about gardening because I don't know how to care about that at the moment. I don't know what to say about plants, and the weather here is distracting. It's hot as hell outside and a hundred times more humid than Afghanistan. Being outside is like being trapped inside a melting plastic bag.

"I just wanted to show you my garden," says my mother. "I've been working hard on it since you went overseas." She shrugs at the tomatoes, unsure of what else to add, but clearly thinking something over. We don't know how to talk to each other since I've returned. I have to train myself to stop thinking about things that aren't here, that I have no control over now. I can't stop thinking about the militia house. If I could think about something else, I would. The wooden fence bordering our yard behind her could be the wall of a room in the militia house. The grass is the concrete floor covered in piles of jackal shit and porcupine quills. I look up at the sky because that's the only place I can't see it.

"Thank you for showing me," I say. My mother smiles and starts watering the plants. The blue notebook pops into my head and I remember the story about the silverware when I was a kid, so I ask my mother if she remembers telling the story. She hesitates, thinking about it, and finally tells me she must have set the silverware back on the counter herself. It couldn't have been a ghost, she tells me. She was just grieving at the time and not her usual self. I thought I would have gotten more out of her on the topic, but I guess not.

I go back inside and I lower the blinds in front of my window to help cool the room down and I sleep off the hangover until the sound of a door opening downstairs wakes me up. It's Claire coming home from school. I get up and take a long shower and then I convince her to take me to get ice cream. I tell her she can show off her new driving skills since she did not have her driver's license when I last saw her. I don't know if she really wants to hang out with me, but it's an excuse for her to get the car. Claire agrees to drive, which is nice because I haven't spent any time driving in months. I recline back in the seat because her driving makes me nervous and also because I can't help myself from scanning the road like I'm on a convoy looking for signs of possible IEDs.

I have trouble deciding what type of ice cream to get

because the list of flavors on the menu goes on forever. *Brownie, Butterfinger, chocolate chip, cookie dough, fudge bits, gummy bears, Heath Bar, M&M's, Nestlé, Kit Kat, Twix, apple, banana, blueberry, cherry, strawberry, pineapple, raspberry, wild cherry, butterscotch, caramel, cheesecake, coconut, fudge, Hershey's, marshmallow, oatmeal cookie, Oreo, peanut butter, peppermint Teddy Grahams, waffle cone pieces, whipped cream.* It's exhausting. I wait for Claire to order and repeat exactly what she says so I don't have to think about it, then I pay the cashier for both of us.

"How's school?" I ask when we finally sit down with our ice cream. I can't think of anything else to ask her. We used to have Bryce as a buffer between us, the middle child who added a sense of balance. For some reason that made things easier. Now I don't know. I don't know what normal people want to talk about, let alone high school girls.

"It's boring," she says, not looking up from her ice cream. "And easy."

"Sorry about last night," I say. I don't want to hear any more details about whatever I did last night, but I can judge from my headache and her attitude towards me that it wasn't good. I don't want to hear stories about being wasted. I hate thinking about myself like that. It's embarrassing to imagine anyone from the platoon seeing me like that. Not just the lieutenant, but the junior marines too. As soon as I'm away from them I go and make an ass of myself, exactly what they'd expect.

"You know," she says, unable to hold it back any longer. "It's not our fault if everything sucks, but you act like it is. Like I'm the one who has to pick you up after Tyler texts me? I'm sixteen. I'm not even supposed to be driving alone that late. You're lucky no one heard me take the car."

"Yeah, I'm sorry," I say.

"You cried the whole way home, by the way. You're lucky no one heard you when we got back home too."

"Okay, I get it," I say before she can keep going. "I meant it when I said I was sorry. I won't be like that again."

Claire takes a scoop of ice cream in her spoon and closes her mouth over it. I don't really want mine anymore, but I eat it because I paid for it. It's cold and sweet and I think I could have said any random combination of flavors to the cashier and the experience would be the same regardless. The idea of ice cream was more alluring when I was in Afghanistan and couldn't get any. I change the subject so I ask if Claire knows who Nicki Minaj is.

"Everyone does," she says.

"Yeah," I say. I realize when we were in Leatherneck I probably could have tried to buy a bootleg CD at the bazaar. People were buying all kinds of shit there. I ask her if she'll drive us to the store to get the new Nicki Minaj CD after we're done eating. The Nicki Minaj CD? What am I even talking about? It sounds like a stupid request, but I'm trying to be normal.

"Normal people don't buy CDs," she says. "They download everything."

"Who said I was normal?" I say, and she laughs at that. All I know about normal is that I haven't experienced it in a while. "Can you take me anyway? We're already out and I don't want to go back home yet. I just want to go to a store and spend money."

"I need to do homework," she says. "But okay." I wish I knew her better and we could spend time together without me feeling like I'm wasting her time. I'm afraid that if I talk to my sister more about school, then I'll just sound like a parent.

Plus, what the fuck do I know about school? I dropped out. She shouldn't take my advice even if I had any to give.

We toss our empty, soggy cardboard cups into a waste-basket and walk back to the car in the parking lot. My lips are numb from the cold ice cream. Some of the moments from the previous night come back to me. I remember see-ing Natalie's face in the crowd, but I try to brush that image out of my head. She's at school about two hundred miles away from here, maybe even graduated by this point if she came through on her plan to finish early. I haven't stayed in touch with her, so I don't know. I don't need to think about that. I take a breath after climbing into the passenger seat and buckling in, then I recline the seat again so I can't see the road. It's a silent car ride once more. We're going to buy music, but we don't listen to any during the ride. I pretend to be asleep at first, then I actually fall asleep again. I wake up when the car stops moving.

Claire drops me off in the parking lot, near the front door, and then drives down one of the aisles to park the car. Yet another first for me is going back into a big retail store filled with people. It's weird to see parents with their kids walking around. I haven't seen a typical family or any children for a while, not even at the airport when I landed. Am I supposed to smile and wave at people, or just ignore them? The fluo-rescent lights in the store take my eyes a minute to get used to. The only comparison I have to a large open space like this from recent memory is the big transient tents we lived in at Leatherneck, or the inside of the main chow hall. But those places were mostly dark on the inside. This store is lit up as bright as possible. I wait around for Claire to walk in, but it doesn't seem like she's going to be here anytime soon, so I decide to walk off and look on my own.

At least they have signs hanging from the ceiling to show me where to find everything. It helps me pretend to look like I know what I'm doing. Appliances to my left. To my right are the computer and mobile sections. Video games beyond that, and then I see the music sign hanging straight in front of me, the most obvious location. Some guy in a blue polo and khakis asks if I need any help. I probably look like a lost tourist or like I'm planning a robbery.

"Just browsing," I say as I walk past him across the carpeted floor. I don't need someone's help sorting through an alphabetical index, even if he's just really good at the alphabet. When I get to the music section it's like the CD aisle goes on for miles. Maybe I should have allowed the blue polo to help me out after all. I walk along the ranks of plastic CD cases to find the artists in the M section, but there aren't any Nicki Minaj CDs there. There isn't even a label for her name. I flip through the plastic-wrapped cases and don't find anything. I walk back to the N artists, and there's also nothing there, not even close. I didn't expect this to be complicated.

Before I move on, it dawns on me how stupid this all is. How does someone fail at finding a pop music CD in a big-box retail store? Even considering it a failure feels stupid, like there was ever the possibility of achieving some type of success in the first place, going home and claiming a small victory as if I had conquered an obstacle. Everyone is still back in Afghanistan. They're still working twelve-hour shifts, going on convoys, working their asses off. I'm in a damn store trying to buy some bullshit music album because being in a war makes you feel like you're missing out on everything in the real world. I don't know what else to do other than try to catch up with everyone.

I go back to get the blue polo and I tell him I need help

after all. He walks with me to the music section like someone holding my hand as we cross the street. I watch him flip through the stacks of CDs over and over again, just as I had done moments before. He doesn't come up with anything.

"Hm," he says when he doesn't find Nicki Minaj. "That's strange. We should have it." He checks both the *M* and *N* sections. He logs on to a computer at the end of the CD rack and scrolls through some Web pages. Then Claire walks up behind me right about when the guy says he can't find anything in their computer system. Claire throws her hands out, frustrated that she even came inside.

"Very odd," he says. "I would normally be able to order this for in-store pickup, but I think I'm going to have to let our IT people know we have a problem with the system. I can't apologize enough for this. I don't have the necessary access to fix anything."

"This is why everyone just downloads music," Claire says. She's within earshot of the employee, but he pretends not to hear her. I could tell him I don't have time for this, but I'm polite about it. I tell him thanks anyway and Claire drives me back home. I get on the family computer and make an account on iTunes and I type in at least fifteen different searches before I give up and then I wonder if I misheard the name of the artist, but that couldn't be because Claire and the employee both knew who I was talking about. Nothing I try seems to work, no matter what I do. If Nicki Minaj isn't even real, then I've wasted a bunch of time, but that would mean everyone is in on the same joke. I don't want to ask for help, but I finally give up. I ask Claire, doesn't she already have it downloaded? She says no. It's not her type of music.

XLV

My phone starts buzzing as I sit at the computer. I roll back from the desk and reach into my pocket, but it's an unknown number, so I push one of the shoulder buttons on the phone and put it back in my pocket. I'm not curious enough to answer and I'm not really in the mood to talk to any strangers. They'll leave a message if it's important enough. I'm too frustrated to talk to anyone. I scoot the chair back to the desk and I log off the computer. Then before I can stand up, the same call comes through again, another call labeled UNKNOWN. It would be a crazy coincidence if it wasn't the same caller again. I ignore it, pushing one of the shoulder buttons to silence the phone again. I have no idea who would be calling. It would have to be telemarketing or a wrong number. I just reactivated my phone a couple days ago and barely anyone knows I'm back in the States. Not even all of my extended family knows. No one would know my number has been activated other than the friends and family who know I'm home, and there's not many who do. No one leaves a voicemail after either of the calls.

The sun is still up. I watch the backyard trees through

the window next to the computer monitor. Their leaves sway in the wind like hands grasping for something just out of reach. My eyelids droop as I verge on passing out. I haven't done anything strenuous today, but I'm ready to fall asleep. My father is at the office late and my mother left to go to her yoga class after Claire and I got home with the car. There's no reason for me to stay awake on anyone else's behalf if they're all busy anyway. They all have other things to do. I've barely seen my own family since coming home, but I guess we still have time to catch up before the rest of the battalion returns to the States. You'd think they'd be more excited to have me home.

I haven't had dinner yet. I'm hungry enough to eat, but at the same time I have no appetite. I don't know what that means. Maybe my stomach is adjusting from the food I ate in Afghanistan to the food I'm now eating. Maybe I'm just too anxious to eat. Everything about my life here is different, even my own thoughts. There are so many things happening at once. I try not to worry about it while I go upstairs and take another one of the long showers I've been taking since I got home. When I come out of the bathroom and close my bedroom door, I see another missed call on my phone from UNKNOWN. A third call? No sooner do I pick the phone up then it starts buzzing again for the fourth attempt. This time I answer it.

"Hello?"

"Trash Six-Four, Dwyer flight line," says a voice. I laugh right away because it's obviously someone fucking with me, calling from the company office using those prepaid AT&T calling cards that everyone mails in care packages. I know it's a joke because *Trash* is the radio call sign for the C-130 squadron we worked with at Leatherneck. Camp Dwyer

is a base south of there with a lot of flights back and forth
between the two fixed-wing runways. I wait for whoever is
on the other end to give up the game so we can share a laugh
about it.

"Trash Six-Four, Dwyer flight line," the voice says again.
The voice comes through a bit garbled and fuzzy, but the
phones in-country are landline connections. The call should
be coming through clear with a landline, shouldn't it?

"Very funny," I say. "Who is this?" The static on the other
end builds for a moment and then fades like a rolling wave. I
think about the other marines who I worked with at Leatherneck. It could be one of them calling to fuck with me, maybe
Melton. It's a possibility at least, so I ask again who's there.

"Radio check, over," the broken voice says. I squeeze the
phone in my hand. I wasn't sure about anything at first, but
now I'm pretty sure the voice belongs to Vargas. How is he
dialing into a phone call if he's using a radio? What the fuck?
This makes about as much sense as everything else. I decide
to play along for now.

"Uh, broken but readable," I say, and then, "Vargas?" The
voice, maybe Vargas, doesn't react.

"Standby," he says. A moment goes by without any voice
at all, just the static.

"Vargas," I say. "You there? Radio check." I say his name
again, but there's no answer. "Vargas, it's Loyette. Where
are you?" I listen carefully. Whatever comes next, I want to
make sure I understand. I hear him breathing or struggling
to breathe. The low breaths are distinct within the static.
Then Vargas speaks, but the low breathing continues behind
his voice.

"Where am I?" he says, reflecting my question back. "I'm
here."

"Are you in the basement?" I ask, not knowing what else to call it. "Is Johnson with you? What do you see?" At first, it's only the crackling radio sounds that answer. Then I hear Vargas sniffling, crying maybe. It's hard to tell through the static.

"At first, you'll see nothing, and then you'll wish you had seen nothing," whispers Vargas. "It is what it is."

"Vargas, listen to me," I say. "Where are you? What does that mean?"

A faint puff of air blows against my ear and I toss my phone across the room and it lands on the carpet in the corner. No way, I think. Impossible. It's just the power of suggestion, like a photo of a spider making an arachnophobe sensitive to the slightest touch. No one breathed through the phone because air can't travel through phone lines. But also, who was breathing in the background?

I'm just too stressed, that must be it. That's the only explanation other than Vargas still being trapped in the militia house. And maybe the militia house is putting him in touch with me for some reason. That's the only guess I have, but he's still alive. That's for sure. It was his voice. I don't know where to start or who to get in touch with. Should I call someone? Who would be the appropriate point of contact for this? I go back to the computer and log on to Facebook, but I can't find anyone's account. I search the names of the marines in my platoon, but no one shows up. I search more names, the others from outside my platoon who I know from the company and the battalion, but I find nothing. I can't find anyone from my permanent unit either, none of my friends or NCOs. I search Red and Arnold, just like we promised we would when we all got back home. But it doesn't work. There's no search result.

I know I should report the phone call to someone in my chain of the command. It's the responsible thing to do, what would be expected of me. I have to tell someone that I've heard from Vargas, or that I think I might have. If there's no way for me to reach anyone online, then I have to find some other way to send a secure communication through the Marine Corps to the personnel deployed overseas, and I don't know where to begin with that. I don't have access to my SIPR account from home, so I can't send any secure messages to the lieutenant. I don't really know the proper way to contact my unit directly, and I've never needed to know because I'm always with them. There aren't any USMC bases within hundreds of miles. I can only think of one place nearby that would qualify as a military installation: the local recruiting station. It's too late now, so I'll have to wait until tomorrow for them to open. I struggle to sleep all night, unable to get the image out of my head of Johnson's boots disappearing into the sea of porcupine quills, unable to get the sound of the mysterious breathing out of my head.

XLVI

The recruiting office hasn't changed one bit since I was last here. The walls are adorned with posters, memorabilia, framed awards given to the recruiters during their early military careers. I signed up at this exact recruiting office, just over two years ago now, a full lifetime. The only thing different is the people. None of the sergeants or staff sergeants are familiar to me. They sit at their desks around the perimeter of the room in their dress blue delta uniforms with short-sleeved khaki shirts and bright blue pants with red stripes down the seam. Some of the recruiters talk on landline telephones; others sit across their desk from high school kids contemplating one of the most important decisions they'll ever make. If only I could warn them all.

The walls are plastered with the historical figures and battles we learned about and memorized in boot camp. *Chesty Puller. Dan Daly. Smedley Butler. Opha May Johnson. Carlos Hathcock. Tun Tavern. Iwo Jima. Inchon. Khe San. Hue. Fallujah. Honor. Courage. Commitment.* All of it. This is the only place locally where I know I will find marines. Someone here has to know how to contact my chain of command directly, without some kind of civilian intermediary. They have to know how. This would be a lot easier if I could just call the company office in Delaram, but you have to receive the call from them. There's no way to dial into those phones from here.

For a second, I fake myself out into thinking Staff Sergeant Rynker is in the recruiting office. A staff sergeant glances at me from the far end of the open office. His face and haircut look identical until he turns sideways and reveals his profile to look nothing like Staff Sergeant Rynker. Maybe coming here is a mistake. If it turns out they can't help me, then I'll feel like a fool. I freeze up for a moment, turning back towards the parking lot. There's a clear view through the window of strip malls and department stores outside, and then the interstate beyond. Shit. I put my hand on the door, ready to push it back open.

"Hey there, killer," a recruiter says from behind me. "What can I do for you?" He's the only one at his desk not in mid-conversation with someone. His desk sits closest to the door, next to the red pull-up bar set up over a circular rug with the Marine Corps emblem printed on it. Just being here makes me feel like a recruit again, like a kid. I walk across the carpet and take a seat at one of the two chairs set up in front of his desk. His white barracks cover sits on a cleared-off portion of his desk. It would be a mere decoration if he wasn't required to wear it while outdoors. Pinned to his chest is a rainbow rectangle of ribbons stacked in four rows. I can see with a quick glance that he's been to Iraq twice. He's been awarded the Navy Achievement Medal. I fold my hands on my lap, then I rest one hand on each knee, then I fold them again.

"Uh, good morning, Staff Sergeant," I say. The black

name tag with white letters pinned above his right breast pocket reads SMITH. I ask about my old recruiter to break the ice.

"His three years were up a few months ago and he shipped to Okinawa," Staff Sergeant Smith says. He touches his chin with his thumb and forefinger, narrowing his eyes. I can tell he's checking my haircut. Anyone in the Marines could see that my haircut is intended to be a medium reg, but whether it's short enough is always up to the nearest authority figure. Staff Sergeant Smith reaches across the desk to shake my hand as he officially introduces himself.

"Corporal Loyette, by the way," I say and the recruiter raises an eyebrow.

"Loyette, Alex?"

"Yes, Staff Sergeant."

"No shit," he says. "I've heard about your hero brother. Bruce was it?"

"Bryce," I say, reflecting on the word *hero* as I nod. It's been a while since I've heard someone call him that. He's dead, so of course he's a hero. My brother stepped on an IED during my second year of college. If that's all it takes, then it's technically not as difficult to become a hero as everyone makes it out to be.

"Semper Fi. Good to have a marine from the fleet in here for a change," he says. "Too much brass snooping around if you ask me, too many kids. You know we still got your brother's picture up there with the others." He points to the back of the office where they've got a bulletin board covered with official portrait photos taken of every kid from this recruiting station who enlisted and then graduated from boot camp, a little bulletin board of honor.

"So what can I do for you, killer?"

I unfold my hands and rest my elbows on the chair's arm-rests. My fingers search around for something to grab hold of, but there's nothing. The other recruiters shoot me side-ways glances amidst their sales pitches given to high school kids, lying to them about how much they'll get laid after they enlist, or telling half truths about the financial benefits to people who are too young to understand the importance of health insurance or an interest-free home loan from the VA. I try to think of how I could explain what's going on. *What do I even explain?* I start off by telling the recruiter that I got sent home from my deployment early, then I go from there. While I talk, he rests his elbows on the desk and folds his hands under his chin, tilting his head to the side as if it helps him hear me better. I tell him someone in my platoon is missing and I might have heard from him.

"I need to contact my unit, but I didn't know where else to go," I say.

"Why haven't you contacted your family readiness offi-cer about this, Devil? Seems to be the obvious course of action from what I'm hearing." He's talking about the civil-ian who maintains contact between other civilians and their deployed family members. I have no idea who the family readiness officer is in our battalion. I'm sure I was introduced to them in a briefing at some point, but I don't remember.

"I don't think what I have to say is for civilian ears, Staff Sergeant," I say, hoping he understands what I mean, that I'm trying not to violate operational security by keeping everything as in-house as possible.

"What do you mean?" he asks.

I go into some of the basic details, about how Vargas dis-appeared from the FOB and we went to look for him and then got lost. I start explaining how I was rescued, but the recruiter holds up a hand to stop me. It all sounds just as crazy to me as I hear myself say it out loud. It feels ridiculous to explain it, so I'm almost glad he stops me because I don't want to sound like an idiot.

"Is this even something I should be hearing?" he says. He's not interested in dealing with this, I think. It's a responsibility he doesn't want to take on. There's no computer at his desk, but there's a stack of Post-its and a cup full of pens that he has not used to take notes as I speak.

"I need to tell someone in my unit that I heard from him, so they know he's alive at least. I can't just sit here and do nothing."

"Look," he says. "First time I came home from Iraq, nothing made sense to me either. I was a son of a bitch to my wife, a son of a bitch to my kids, and a son of a bitch to my dog." I notice he's not wearing a wedding ring. "Adjusting takes time," he says. "You can't force it, killer. You just have to calm down and be patient and work on it, okay? I get what you're going through. Just try to relax and enjoy your time at home."

"I'm not making this up, Staff Sergeant. I need to get in touch with my command."

"Then you need to call the FRO," the recruiter says again. "That's how you contact your command. You can't come in here and kick up a shitstorm because you're confused about the way things work. You need to follow the process. It's your job to know your chain of command, not mine. We've got a job to do here and sadly it isn't tracking down phone numbers. I'm not a phone operator. And for all I know you could just be fucking with me, so I'm out on this one, sorry. There's a FRO for a reason. Call them."

"I'm not fucking with you, Staff Sergeant."

He glances at the potential recruits seated around the room, checking to see if they're listening, and he looks back at me and sighs. "Look, you're a damn hero in my book. Anyone shooting camel jockeys in Afghan is a hero in my book. You're young enough to be wasting time in college studying interpretive dance or history or some bullshit like that, but you're doing something with your life instead, and I respect that. We need more people like you around. You're good to go, but I'm not about to get caught up in something that's not my business, whether you're for real or not about any of this trash. It is what it is," says the recruiter. "Check your unit website and find the phone number for the FRO. It's always listed there. Hell, your parents probably have it written down somewhere. They always contact families with all that info before deployments, got it? Now if that's it, I need to get back to work, Devil."

"Good to go, Staff Sergeant," I say, thinking about what it is that I'm doing with my life. I tell him to have a good day before I leave.

XLVII

I sit down at the computer when I get home and I search for my battalion on the internet. There are no helpful results. All I find is a page with the address of battalion HQ at Camp Lejeune, no emails, not even a phone number. I guess I'll have to see if any contact info for the family readiness officer was provided to my parents. I hear the car pulling out of the driveway outside, which means my mother is headed out somewhere. My father is already at work. My sister is at school. I check through drawers and files, but I don't find anything helpful. I don't have a way to go very far with both my parents' cars gone, and I don't know where I would go if I could. Tyler could pick me up if he has the day off work, but I don't think hanging out with him again is a good idea right now.

It's still morning, but I'm as tired as I would be at the end of a full day of hard work. Lying awake all of last night has taken its toll, so I log off the computer and head upstairs to sleep until everyone comes home later. I reach the second floor and I see Bryce's bedroom door partially open as I walk to my room, which is unusual because no one ever goes in there now. There's no need to poke around in there. I pull the door closed without looking inside and then I go back to my room and pass out on my bed.

I smell food cooking when I wake up. It's not dark out yet, but I can see the orange hue of early evening sunlight through the window, so it must be dinnertime. I've slept all day, not realizing I would be out that long. I check my phone to find no missed calls or text messages waiting for me, then I set it on the nightstand and walk downstairs. I suppose now is finally the moment for me and my family to spend some time together for once. My mother and father are both in the kitchen getting dinner ready. My father is still in a shirt and tie because he says he has to go back to the office later. Something I've learned about him throughout my life is if he's wearing a collared shirt, no matter what time of the day it is, then he's still at work. The doorbell rings before I can ask him what's so important at the office that he needs to leave again.

"Go ahead and answer it," my mother says with a smile, as if there's a big surprise waiting for me. It turns out the surprise is a special dinner guest. I open the door and find my uncle, Hank, waiting out front. He's my mother's brother, so his smile is nearly identical to hers. I try to look excited to see him, but I wish my parents would have told me he was coming beforehand. I liked Uncle Hank better when I was a kid, but now all he wants to do is talk about politics and ask me about being enlisted. It doesn't help that he's also a veteran.

He walks through the door and encloses me in a hug and claps his hand on my back a few times. Hank was in the Air Force in Vietnam, so he gets a big hard-on for other military people. You can tell he wasn't drafted. He's probably the only person in my family who was excited to hear about my enlistment at the time. Everyone else was worried, but he told me it was the right thing to do for my country after what happened to Bryce. He'll probably have an endless list of questions for me about Afghanistan. I can deal with him for now unless he's staying for longer than just dinner.

My parents tell me to wait in our stuffy dining room after I let them know Hank has arrived. They tell me I'm the guest of honor and they don't want me lifting a finger to do anything. I sit at the table while my family carries in the food and I wonder why someone would design a dining room with no windows. I feel like I can't take a full breath of air in here as they set down the plates of food. There's a green bean casserole, mashed potatoes, chicken, meat loaf. There's red wine. It's like an early Thanksgiving dinner.

Hank insists that he say grace before we eat, and he recites a rhyming prayer about eating food and being thankful. During the prayer, I think about Vargas whispering each night, praying as he told me that one time. Had he been saying the same thing all along, or only after we went inside the militia house? You'll wish you had seen nothing. Hank finishes the prayer by adding a thank-you note about me coming home safely and then we start eating. We drink the wine, even Claire. It doesn't take long for the alcohol to hit me like it has been recently.

"Shit," I say when I notice the room swimming. I've only finished one glass.

"Alex," says my mother. "Watch the TV-14 language." Claire laughs at that.

"Come on," says Hank. "Kid's a hero. Let him be." He says some other shit about earning my right to do things other people haven't earned the right to do, a validation of my outdated thought process from when I first enlisted two years ago. Back then I thought if I joined the Marines, no one would care that I was about to fail out of school; instead they would think I was doing something more important, contributing to a cause bigger than myself. If I enlisted, then no one would question me for neglecting the important goals in life such as getting good grades so I could get a good job and get married and buy a house. I ran away from my own lost cause only to get saddled with another that has been ongoing since I was in grade school. Where has it gotten me since then? I could have bypassed all of this if only I had taken charge of my life while I had the chance.

My father sits at the table to my left, his tie knot loosened, the top button of his collar undone. He finishes chewing and then speaks, waving the fork around in his hand with his elbow resting on the white tablecloth. Claire sits between us, so he leans out in front of her to look at me directly.

"So, Alex," he says amidst the sound of everyone's metal silverware clinking against their dinner plates. "Do we ever get the full story? About why you ended up home sooner than expected? I don't think we did. Can't you tell us more about anything?"

"I can't really," I say. "I don't want to get in trouble."

"That sounds ominous."

"Pete," my mother says, shooting him a glance.

"What, Linda?" says my father. "I think it's fair to ask."

"I'm not trying to be ominous," I say. "I just don't want to get in trouble."

"Secret agent," my father says. "What *can* you tell us? Come on. You always liked to tell stories when you were growing up, right?" He scoops another mouthful of food from his plate and forks it into his mouth. Sometimes I forget that everyone back home had been reading my blog about Afghanistan, including my parents. My father rests on his elbows and continues looking at me. I try to ignore him. I don't like when conversations about me are at my expense.

"How come you never ask me to tell you stories?" Hank asks.

"Because we never have to ask," says my father, which makes Hank laugh.

I tell them a little bit, that my job is boring, which is mostly true. My father lets it go after I trail off and Hank asks Claire about high school. They talk about extracurricular activities and applying to college scholarships. My head hangs over my plate. I slide my empty glass towards my mother for more wine, but she doesn't refill it. Hank grabs the bottle and fills it for me and my mother scowls at him. I drink the glass in two gulps and slide it back towards Hank, my new buddy.

"Alex," Claire says, and I laugh without looking at her. I don't want to be sober anymore.

"We'll take care of him," Hank says, pouring me more wine. He's sitting across from me, but he doesn't look me in the eye. Maybe there was a time when he was a clean-cut Airman First Class in his sharp uniform. Now he's bald and out of shape like my father. He keeps a pair of aviators on nearly all the time, either pulled down over his eyes or propped up at the top of his head. He asks me what it's like *over there*. Everyone else here has been too afraid to ask in direct terms like that.

"You don't have to say too much if you aren't at liberty," Hank says. "I'm just curious about it is all."

"Well," I say. I gulp down more wine. "It's dirty. It's cold. Then it's hot. Then it's cold. But mostly hot."

A fly buzzes over the table and my father swats at it. Hank nods and says it sounds familiar. He feels this camaraderie with me that I don't feel at all. He and I are *brothers in arms* in his eyes. We're related by blood, which is enough of a connection for me. I don't need anything more than that. I keep eating to pass the time. The food smells like food. It looks like my mother's cooking, but it doesn't taste like her cooking. It tastes like salt and air. I tell Hank to mail me candy and socks next time I'm deployed.

"Well, thank God you're here now," he says. "I won't need to mail it. I can just hand it over next time I come by to visit."

"No," I say. A second fly joins the first. I imagine my dirty M16, gooey with lubricant and dust. I want to tell Hank we need washing machines for our rifles since all we have are rags and toothbrushes, but I laugh instead of saying anything else. The walls are plain with nothing hanging on them, not even a mirror.

"Are you sure you can't tell us about anything else?" my father says again. "Absolutely sure? I've been curious for such a long time now. Only if you're at liberty, of course. We didn't hear much from you while you were gone."

"My friends disappeared in a basement," I say, setting my silverware on the table. "We went into this piece-of-shit building that's haunted and full of dog shit and I don't know if anyone's going to find them, ever, and it's my fault that they're gone. And now I'm eating mashed potatoes and no one knows where they are." I say this as I slop mashed potatoes onto my plate and then I keep going. "At first, I saw nothing," I say, spooning mashed potatoes in my mouth. "Now that I have, I wish I hadn't." It occurs to me that I still need to ask about the family readiness officer, but when I look up to ask, I notice everyone is looking at me, their heads turned towards me.

I finish the rest of my wine and I chew on green beans

while they stare. My story is so ridiculous I expect them to take it as a joke, but no one laughs. The two flies buzz near our plates. My father leans forward and grins at me. He finishes chewing and swallows the rest of the food in his mouth. The other members of my family set their silverware down on their plates. My mother and Uncle Hank exchange a look and each of them nods.

"What," I say.

"You know," says my father. "I think you should show some more respect when you talk about the militia house."

The others nod. More flies gather over the table. No one tries to stop me as I excuse myself. No one follows me as I back out of the dining room. My cell phone and the extra set of car keys are in my bedroom, so I head upstairs. I don't know what to do, but I can't stay here tonight. I walk by Bryce's bedroom door on the way to my room. It's partially open again, but no one has gone upstairs since I closed it. The stick figure from our house at the FOB is drawn on the wall next to Bryce's door, pointing towards the opening. I back up and turn on the hallway light and the drawing is gone.

The door creaks as I push it open the rest of the way. Inside the room, the big red Marine Corps flag is still thumb-tacked to the wall. A framed boot camp headshot hangs next to it. Bryce looks extremely young in the picture, like a child, just like I do in mine. The first picture in uniform makes everyone look that way. I don't find anything unusual in the room at first. Nothing else has changed. Bryce's bed waits for him to unmake it. A green seabag filled with his gear sits in the corner. No one has ever opened it. It's filled with things no one wants to sort through.

I'm not just drunk off of wine. Something isn't right.

I've eaten more than enough food every day, but I'm still hungry. No one seems to listen to me. I can't focus on anything. Now I see the top drawer of Bryce's dresser is partially open. I don't remember anything being left that way, half-open so carelessly like that. I open the drawer the rest of the way to find it completely full of porcupine quills, banded in black and white, twice the length of a pencil. They smell like animal shit. I hold my breath when I turn around and see that the combination lock on the green seabag is somehow unlocked now and resting on the floor, the seabag open and stuffed with porcupine quills, overflowing with them.

XLVIII

I walk back downstairs and there are flies everywhere. I hear nothing but flies. No one has moved from their seats in the dining room. They're just sitting there doing nothing, staring across the table at each other. I wave my hands through the cloud of flies on my way to the kitchen and out the patio door. They scatter in the outside air and I'm able to move around without protecting my face. Leaves cover the concrete patio and the grass. The sun has already set below the tree line. Shafts of orange light peek through the branches. I wait at the edge of the forest as no one comes to close the patio door. Everyone inside is still in the dining room. Footsteps echo from the trees, the sound of boots on a solid floor. I turn towards the sound and start moving.

There's no clear trail to follow out here, so I have to push my way through branches and low-lying plants. Vines wrap around my ankles and thorns tear at my skin as I scramble among the shadows cast by the trees. I keep moving forward through the woods. I remember getting lost in these exact woods as a kid, having to call out and listen to the direction of my father's voice to find my way home. Now I'm following a sound that might not even be real.

The footsteps echo once more. Then the ground changes in front of me. The brown dirt washes out beneath the green vines and gives way to ground covered in tan dust. Each step I take causes dust to puff into the air. The green thins out along the dusty earth. The grass and the plants disappear until all that's left is an open clearing in the woods surrounding the militia house. I look back through the trees and my house is still there. The militia house is here too. Nothing about it has changed. The windows are all broken out and the square frames reveal only shadows inside, the same as when we first saw it. Shadows of tree branches spill across the walls as the sun dips lower. I wait and listen, but there's nothing to hear except the birds in the forest around me. I hear the footsteps again, echoing from deep inside. I turn back to look at my house again, but I can no longer see it through the trees. In its place, the forest seems to go on forever.

XLIX

The first-deck hallway of the militia house appears just like it
did when we first explored it. It's full of dirt and animal shit
and it smells awful. A gentle breeze catches a piece of plastic wrapper on the floor. Pockmarks have been chipped out
of the walls by gunfire from a war fought decades before we
came here. The stairway branches off into two options: up or
down. Upstairs are the rooms where the Soviets were killed.
Downstairs is the darkness. The stairs lead to an empty place
where the sun cannot reach. Behind me, the forest is gone and
there is only a dividing line between the brown earth and the
blue sky, a mirage shimmering on the horizon. It never ends.
My house is there this time, just a slight outline in the air. Or
maybe I'm imagining it, hoping it's there. Or dreading that
it might be. My family is gone, but what if they weren't? Then
what? I try to run. I can't move, but this isn't a dream. I'm
wide awake and my mouth is full of dust until it is suddenly
full of flies. I can't breathe. I lose my balance and I fall back
through the front door, back outside of the militia house.
The ground is cold and smooth. I don't feel dirt when I slide

my hand across the surface. Then above me, the sky is blank. The militia house is gone. I can't see anything now because there's nothing but black in the basement. I'm still inside. I've been inside this entire time.

L

The soles of my feet are burning. My boots are gone, and it feels like I've been walking on my bare feet for miles. I don't know what happened to my boots. The red moonbeam is on but getting dimmer. It sits out of reach as if I dropped it by accident, but I don't remember doing that. I don't remember anything from down here. All I remember is being home. The light is pointed right at me. I feel something sturdy at my back, a wall I think. Finally, something other than an endless open floor. I groan as I prop myself up against it. There's enough light to see that I'm wearing the same shorts and T-shirt I had worn to dinner, but all of my gear is gone. My mouth is dry and it feels like I haven't eaten in days. I slide away from the wall far enough to grab the moonbeam, then I slide back and prop myself up. I point the light out to my right. The red beam disappears into nothing before I can see if the wall ends. Same thing to my left, but there's a daypack open on the floor, Vargas's daypack. When I reach it, the green logbook is gone, but my blue notebook is back again, good as new. Why wouldn't it be? This time I open it to find all the pages blank. There's still a beanie inside the pack just like there was before, so I take it out and put it on. I call out unanswered, echoless curses and insults. Fuck this place. The space swallows my voice. I might as well be making no noise at all. I scream until my throat burns and then I start coughing and I punch my fists against the floor. This fucking thing made us come down here just so it could starve us? Why? What kind of test is that? How could we have passed? I curl up on the floor with my head resting on the daypack and I pass out, accepting that I never left the militia house to begin with. I shouldn't believe it, but I do. Nothing injured my leg because no one ever found me. I never spoke with the lieutenant, and probably never will. I'll never know what Nicki Minaj sounds like, or if she's real. I'll never see my family again. I won't get the chance to take time and appreciate everything else that's happened back home since arriving in Afghanistan, not unless the artillery battery finds a way down here, and that's if Blount told them where we went, which all depends on how time is passing outside. There's a good chance they haven't started looking for us yet.

LI

An explosion shudders through the floor and wakes me from a deep sleep. I haven't bothered moving from the spot I'm in. I might as well just stay here. Multiple explosions follow the first. Each explosion is like a wooden pile driven into my skull. Then the sound fades into a ringing. All that's left is the rumbling of the explosions coming through the floor and a single tone like the one in my dreams. It's the triple sevens firing from the FOB, not too far away from wherever I am. It must be. Unless I'm nowhere near the FOB; then I don't know what it is. They fire off several more rounds before it all finally stops. I lie still and wait for them to start firing again, but they don't. I have no idea where they are in relation to me, what direction they're in. The feel of the blasts comes from all around. I wonder if there's any *we* left to speak of. Are Johnson and Vargas still down here? Is anyone else? Are they going to find us at all, even if we're dead when they do? If anyone finds Johnson down here, I don't think they'll like what they find. I hope I'm wrong. There's no food left, so that's it. There's nothing I can do but lie here and wait until I pass out again. It is what it is. At least there's no one here to stop me from sleeping like there is everywhere else. You're never allowed to sleep. I want to sleep, but my insides ache with hunger. I think about what Claire said, that no one made me come here. Or rather, what the house said to me through Claire if that's how this all works. I never really spoke to Claire, but she's right even if she wasn't real. No one made me join the Marines or come to Afghanistan. I chose both of those. All of this has been worthless. I would have never known the truth if I hadn't come here with a gun like people have been doing since before I was old enough to enlist. Since before I was born. No one back home knows what it's like here because they weren't as desperate as I was. They're all so lucky they can ignore everything. I wish I was like them. But now I'm stuck here, and I'll never be able to tell them what it's like. They'll keep living their busy, important lives forgetting there's a war happening here. I can't move. I can't move and it's too late. Too late for everything. There's nowhere to go. Nothing else to think about. I wish the militia house would send me somewhere else again, somewhere good, just one last time.

LII

The explosions stop and I leave the moonbeam on instead of turning it off to save battery. Just in case there's ever something to see down here. I don't have my watch anymore, so I don't know how much time passes by as I lie on the floor. I hear footsteps again, but not a pair of boots. Then I see a dog. It's the same dog Blount and I found at the back gate. The porcupine quills are gone now, leaving dark suggestions of scabs across the dog's face. I reach up and the dog sniffs my hand and licks my fingers. Then the explosions start again and the dog lets out a startled squeak before cowering on the floor and curling up against me. The triple sevens keep firing and the dog presses into me, sharing some of its body heat as it trembles. The dog smells bad, but the warmth is soothing. I don't know why it occurs to me, but I realize our mission in Kajaki is now fully complete. We've done our jobs for the people in charge. We've done what they told us to do. There's nothing we've left undone. The sound of the triple sevens means we did everything right. We did what was asked of us to get the job done here and now the militia house is making us pay for it. I rest one of my arms along the dog's crusty fur. Its breaths come in and out in short gasps. Was the dog down here all along or did it find its way down here through the basement door? Is there another way out we haven't seen? I don't know if it makes any difference. At this point I'm sure no one is coming. I've made peace with that and I'm trying to surrender to the end now. I have no water or food. If there's a way to crawl out, I could maybe try that. If it wasn't too far away at least. But I wouldn't be able to pull myself the whole distance I covered with Johnson. I don't know how far we walked. I imagine them finding me here resting against this blank wall, my body all dried up and shriveled like a fly in a spider's web. They'll wonder why I'm wearing civilian clothes and they'll wonder where my rifle is and where my helmet and the rest of my gear have disappeared to. They will wonder where Johnson and Vargas are, and they won't find the answer down here. I reach over the dog's shivering body and pull the daypack closer, and I pull out the notebook. There's just enough light to see the paper. I find a pen in the pack, but in the red light I'm unable to tell if the ink is black or blue. It doesn't matter. I open it to the first page, blank. Someone else has been tampering with the notebook since we got here. This time I want to be the one writing something.

LIII

dear anyone,

i'm the one to blame. i could've said no when they asked me
to come here, but i said yes. i knew better. it is what it is. no
one else was wrong. they didn't do anything. i thought the
road led nowhere for me but i was wrong. i couldn't see at
first. i didn't even try but it always led where i needed, not
to this dark basement far away. i chose that. things would
be so different now. i'm sorry. i'm not supposed to be here.
no one is. i would do anything to change things. i would do
anything to make things the way they were before i came
here. i would give anything just to have one more chance.
please let me try. please let me try. i'm sorry i left everyone
behind. i'm sorry i didn't pay any attention. i know you
can hear me. you know these words as i write them because
you know my thoughts. just lie to me again. let me think
i'm somewhere else. i was just following orders. doing what
they told me. i never knew what anything meant until now.
at least i figured out some of it. the marines didn't fix me
they just made me someone else. now these words are all

that's left. i would do everything different. i would change everything. please let me try wait

   the door i feel wind the door is right there i can reach it if i try the door is right in front of me

ACKNOWLEDGMENTS

Thank you to Roxane Gay, Julia Kardon, and Caroline Zancan for believing in me and teaching me how to write a novel. Thank you to everyone behind the scenes at Henry Holt who worked hard to make this book a real thing. Thank you to my creative writing teachers for setting me on the right path, especially Marianne, Don, Brian, Sharon, Ted, Matt, Sean, Alex, Julie, and Mike. Thank you to John Rubins for teaching my first workshop and for writing with me. Thank you to Carey Ford Compton and Diana Clarke for reading more of my writing than anyone else in grad school, and for your encouraging feedback on the earliest incarnation of this tale. Thank you to Jill Quirk, Josh Kaminski, and everyone steering the ship. Thank you to my family, friends, and coworkers for putting up with me as I wrote and rewrote this book. Thank you to my chorus of influences, including Gustav Hasford, Miles Lagoze, Tim O'Brien, Matt Young, Anuradha Bhagwati, Phil Klay, Nico Walker, Maximilian Uriarte, Jeff Clement, Jac Jemc, Shirley Jackson, Mark Z. Danielewski, Henry James, Anne Rivers Siddons, Daniel Kehlmann, Sarah Waters, Jeff VanderMeer, Frank Spotnitz, John Shiban, Vince Gilligan, and Daniel Myrick and Eduardo Sánchez. *The Militia House* is a work of fiction. The real people who kept me alive in Afghanistan were First Lieutenant Copes, Staff Sergeant Doerr, Sergeant Bognar, Corporal Boddy, and the members of *Delta Company, 40 Commando* and *India Battery, 3/12*, who put themselves in harm's way on a regular basis. Thank you forever.

ABOUT THE AUTHOR

John Milas served on active duty in the Marine Corps and deployed to Afghanistan in 2010. He later earned a BA and MFA in creative writing. He lives in Illinois, where he reads, writes, and watches baseball. *The Militia House* is his first novel.